Francesca Petrizzo is from Empoli, Italy. She is
currently an undergraduate at Oxford University.
Memoirs of a Bitch is her first novel.

MEMOIRS OF A BITCH

Francesca Petrizzo

Translated from the Italian by
Silvester Mazzarella

Quercus

First published in Great Britain in 2011 by Quercus

Quercus
21 Bloomsbury Square
London
WC1A 2NS

ISBN 978 0 85738 066 1

10 9 8 7 6 5 4 3 2 1

Typeset by Ellipsis Digital Limited, Glasgow
Printed and bound in Great Britain by Clays Ltd, St Ives plc

. . . it seems only yesterday that the Greek ships gathered at Aulis to inflict destruction on Priam and the people of Troy . . .

Homer: *The Iliad*, Book II, lines 303–306

The bitch. That's what the ship's crew call me. The bitch.

They say it behind my back. But I hear them.

My name's Helen; I was born in Sparta, but I went away for love.

They used to say I was the most beautiful woman in the world.

The minstrels are already making stories about how little I've won and how much I've lost. Lying tales. They weren't there, after all. But I was.

I'm walking on the bridge. Far off, the sun is setting. Day giving way to night. The ship carves a foaming wake on the bronze sea.

Is that the Peloponnese already, that dark crest racing far away beyond the water like a pack of wolves? Men rise and fall like leaves on the trees, rise and fall while the gods stay mute.

The ship glides on across metallic waves.

PART ONE

SPARTA

1

My home was built of gold. Big windows facing the river, copper light on stone floors. My home.

My mother Leda was very beautiful, her hair was spun gold, so my nurse said; her smile the smile of a siren. I had a sister with eyes as sharp as blades. Knives in my flesh if I laughed in front of her. She never laughed: Clytemnestra. Thin and serious, hair like flames above green eyes. Born to rule. The long powerful hands of a strangler. When she wrestled with our brother Castor, she always won. I was the youngest. The little one. My daughter, my mother would call me, though she never suckled me. My daughter. They chose a terrible name for me: Helen, the destroyer. Names have power, as I've learned to my cost. But I knew nothing as a child playing on the paths among the slopes of the olive grove.

Sparta. Land of warriors and contorted olives, of tough men – though my father Tyndareus was gentle. Clytemnestra inherited his flaming hair, which didn't go grey as he got older. I had a halo of fire too, red-gold my nurse Etra called it, singing to me as she combed: she'll be very beautiful, this little girl, very beautiful.

People were scared of me. When I joined the little girls of the court, daughters of ambassadors and warriors, they would circle round me and stare in silence. It's Helen, it's Helen, they would whisper. I discovered much later that the women slaves murmured that I was a daughter of Zeus, insinuating that my mother was an unfaithful wife. Officers of the guard went freely in and out of her rooms and her slave girls would whisper in the ears of the palace ladies. But I understood nothing when the other children didn't want me playing with them. Or when Tyndareus – he was my father, I've always believed that, I've always wanted to believe that – gave me a dog that was found drowned in a pool of water after only a single day in my rooms. No hands came to dry my tears. Helen the destroyer. Even then envy and fear were my poison.

Clytemnestra had no love for me. I was the little one, the precious one. I liked the sun, I liked mirrors. I spent hours and hours in empty rooms, gazing at that image, distorted by metal, of a child who looked like me. Clytemnestra was furious one day when she came on me.

'You're ugly! ugly! ugly! I'll make you ugly!' she screamed. I felt her long strong hands in my hair, on my skin. By the time she left me, lying on the floor, purple and black marks were spreading over my body like evil flowers. Outside the window loomed the heavy shadow of the Peloponnese. The mirror had been thrown to the floor, beside a little girl of eight huddled in a pool of black light.

When my nurse Etra came to fetch me, I met her questions with an obstinate silence. No, I would not tell tales and say who had done it. Clytemnestra's eyes were burning into me. I lifted my chin. No.

My mother shook her head gracefully. 'Childish squabbles,' she sighed, 'do stop crying, Helen.' I had already stopped, but she hadn't noticed. She swept from the room wrapped in the rosy froth of an expensive dress. 'Helen, Helen . . .'

My bruises healed. Clytemnestra's eyes no longer mirrored anything but shadows.

I had two brothers, Castor and Pollux: beautiful twins. When they trained in the palace gymnasium, all Sparta came to watch. Girls giggled and sleeked their hair for their benefit. But my brothers ignored them. They only ever had eyes for each other. When Theseus arrived in Sparta one day from Athens with his friend Pirithous, they received him formally, being heirs to the throne.

'The king and queen are away,' they said.

Theseus the Athenian answered: 'Never mind, I'll stay.'

'You're welcome, Theseus.'

That evening, after the banquet, Theseus came looking for me. I had stayed in the women's quarters and never met this tall, fair, well-built man. Already aged by an iron streak tingeing his temples with grey.

'Come here, child.'

He detected my shyness by the milky light of the moon. So he laughed, and like a street conjuror, dropped to one knee and pulled from under his cloak a fine gold chain and amber pendant. In those days I loved the glitter of jewels. Step by step I came closer to this man waiting there so patiently. The amber sparkled. I hesitated as though a crowd were pushing me back, but the unknown man smiled, his hands open. He was my father's age. When I reached out to touch the amber, he grabbed my wrist and stifled my cries with his cloak, thrusting the bitter taste of cloth into my mouth. I retched, then a blow to the nape of my neck knocked me down into darkness. He left me tied up in his room till morning. Then he calmly took his leave of my brothers, thanking them and complimenting them on their generous hospitality. I can see them now, cockerels smoothing their feathers in the rosy flush of dawn. Pirithous brought the horses round to the front of the palace and they threw me on, wrapped in a cloak, like a common bundle. Bound and gagged, the sister of those waving farewell to Theseus from the palace steps.

After a long ride, the Athenians stopped on an isolated promontory by the sea. Tormented by thirst, I was tied to a tree to watch while they threw dice for me. I was twelve years old. Theseus won. Pirithous swore and went to piss into the sea from the edge of the cliff. Theseus, still with the same reassuring fatherly smile on his full lips, came close and reached out a hand to stroke my cheek: don't be afraid ... I bit his hand in blind fury, banishing fear to the furthest recesses of my heart. His face changed; a father replaced by a furious man. He slapped me hard. The clear sky and the sea beyond the cliff edge from where Pirithous was watching, smiling with amusement, were hidden by the mist in my swollen eyes. But I did not close them even when Theseus straightened up and took off his belt. I struggled to lift my chin one more time in proud defiance, regardless of the fear in my heart. I'm made of stone.

He didn't rape me, Theseus. Before he could do anything a squad of armed horsemen arrived at a furious gallop from Sparta. At their head Castor and Pollux, exhausted and covered with dust. They had followed the tracks left by the Athenians. With a single throw of his spear, one of the soldiers pierced Pirithous to the heart, knocking him over the cliff without a sound.

'We don't want war with Athens: just go,' Castor told Theseus from the back of his horse.

Theseus laughed and lifted his hands: 'She's all yours.' He came to retrieve his cloak from me. 'I'll be back, princess,' he said with a wink. The promise of a rapist. Words to be believed. But he died first, Theseus did. One day the husband of a woman he was in bed with would cut his throat. But on this particular day he left in peace. Wrapped in his cloak like a vagabond. Humming sacred hymns.

My brothers never even dismounted. They gave a sign and one of the soldiers of the guard, a polite young man, got off his horse and cut my bonds with his sword. Then he lifted me in his arms and mounted again, wrapping me in his red wool cape. At a signal from Pollux we started back for Sparta, my brothers joking with each other at the head of the column, never turning to see how I was or even to speak to me.

'I'm thirsty,' I murmured into the folds of the cape. Hearing me, the man pressed his water bottle to my lips at full gallop. The water filled my mouth and spilled on to the cloak, sodden wool sticking to my chest as my tired head fell against his leather breastplate. The world rocked beyond my exhausted eyes. And my exhausted ears sank into sleep to the shrill laughter of my brothers.

2

When my mother came home, she found me in the garden. Alone and silent as always, on the hillside among the olive trees. I was sitting on the ground without any toy or ball. Nothing. Well combed, well dressed, a child who no longer wanted to break anything. Then she understood. Perhaps for a moment, a unique moment, she was with me. She spread her dress on the grass and sat down beside me. Something she had never done before, and would never do again.

'Helen, Helen ...' she murmured, even taking me in her arms. I was still a child, and she pressed my head against her breast and held me close. But I didn't cry. I hadn't cried for some time.

'It won't happen again,' she went on slowly. 'Never again. We'll protect you. We'll find a way. Don't be afraid, Helen.'

I nodded slowly against that breast veiled in purple linen. Her jewels tinkled over my head. I believed her. Children always believe their mothers.

My father redoubled the guards. Visiting strangers were not allowed to see me. 'Just us and only us,' he instructed my mother.

She laughed and ruffled my hair. 'Beauty's not so dangerous.'

'But blood is. She's descended from kings. Never forget that, Leda.'

My mother's eyes narrowed. Clytemnestra's eyes. 'I shan't, don't you worry,' she said, and without touching me again, she left us.

I turned to my father who was sitting on his throne. His chin propped on his hand, he ignored me. That evening the flames in his hair seemed to have gone out. He was smothered in invisible ash.

'Go to bed, Helen,' he said in a slow monotonous voice, like a peasant or a merchant. Not the voice of a king. A common voice suitable for running a family as ordinary as any other. I obeyed, got up and went away.

There was a sentry on guard outside my room. They changed the guard four times a day, soldiers armed ready for combat. Unsleeping, defending my door. I was still having nightmares about Theseus. But I had no one to discuss them with; the sentry outside my door had no authority over the unravelled territory of my dreams. I lay down between the sheets to wait for sleep. It was summer, and a light breeze from the river reached me from the windows. The curtains were billowing like sails. Sleep was singing in the corners of my eyes, but I had to struggle to keep them closed. The wicked leer of Theseus was keeping me awake. If I'd cried out, if I'd shouted for her, Etra would have come to sleep with me. A sentry to guard me from my dreams. But I would not call out. I'm made of stone.

Sleep came, bringing Theseus. The same sky, the same sea. Pirithous falling into space, blood streaming through the air. And no one to stop Theseus unclasping his belt. Closing my eyes was the same as keeping them open. I woke screaming. A noise at my door, and the guard was in the room. Spear raised, dagger unsheathed. A fierce face under his crested helm.

'An intruder, princess?'

I shook my head. 'Just a bad dream.'

An almost inaudible sigh of relief filled the air. He put his dagger away, propped his spear against the wall. Took off his helm: 'Thanks to the gods, princess.' His smile was white in the darkness; his face young and strong.

'You're the man who gave me a drink.'

'It was an honour, princess.' He thumped his chest, picked up his weapons and went back to the door. I was twelve years old. I needed nothing more.

Agamemnon was a greedy man. You didn't notice at first, only later when he thought no one was looking, you would see his beady roving eyes stopping on a painted amphora, a jewel or a particular person. That's what he was like, Agamemnon; he helped himself to whatever he wanted. And he wanted everything. He was ruling Mycenae without a queen, so he came all the way to Sparta to find one.

'I've come on the wings of rumour, Tyndareus,' he announced, planting himself in the middle of the throne room.

For once I'd been allowed to leave my rooms and be seen. But Agamemnon's eyes went past me. Ignored for the first time in my life, I saw them fasten on Clytemnestra like the eyes of a cat. Seeing herself noticed, she smiled. She had pointed triangular canines, my sister; the smile of a wolf. Agamemnon said it was her fame that had brought him all the way to Sparta. The fame of the wolf princess who liked to run through the olive groves in the middle of the night and dive naked into the icy waters of the Eurotas. That was what Clytemnestra was like: relentless. I wasn't. I loved gardens and the warm baths Etra prepared for me. And mirrors. Yes, I was beautiful, but that wasn't enough.

'It's not enough, little sister. Not for a real man. Not enough to appeal to a king. You're insipid, Helen.'

Clytemnestra was changing her clothes in her room. I watched from the bed, enchanted. She let the white peplos she'd been wearing that evening fall to the floor and admired her body with satisfaction in the bronze mirror. She had a lovely figure. The strong physique of an athlete. I was the only woman in Sparta who had never run in the stadium. I had never exercised naked in the mud and dust with boys and girls of my own age. I was delicate; too delicate, Leda said. I thought if her as 'Leda', not as 'my mother'. It was hard to think of calling her that.

Clytemnestra threw down the elegant peplos carelessly and kicked aside the gold pins. Rummaging in the wooden chest, she chose a short tunic, one of those she sometimes used for running.

'You're so beautiful,' she told herself in the mirror, smiling. Clytemnestra brilliant as the moon. I loved her so much. But she didn't know that. She could only imagine ferocious passions, and for me the time for learning about ferocious passions would not come till much later. Perhaps too much later.

She looked over her right shoulder at me: 'Go to bed, go to your own room, brat.'

I tightened my lips.

'Go to bed,' she repeated.

I had no intention of moving. I wanted her to know I was made of stone. She blew out the lamp without giving me another look. From the corners of the room rose a darkness slashed by the rays of the moon.

'I don't want to find you here when I come back.'

Nor did she. I had no need to follow her to know where she was going. I had no need to slip through the shadows of the olive grove to know that Agamemnon was waiting for her. I picked up the white peplos, the universal symbol of virginity, from the floor and took it with me. I kept it rolled in a ball under my pillow until she left. In any case, Clytemnestra never wore a white peplos again. She had no further use for them.

The wedding was six days later. A banquet that went on till dawn. Bride and groom smiling by torchlight under garlands of jasmine. Lips drawn tight over sharp teeth. The usual wolfish leer. Agamemnon's hand a claw round Clytemnestra's shoulder. Asserting ownership. He had placed a gold neckband round her neck. A collar. A beautiful collar for the princess of the wolves, for the athlete who liked diving into the icy Eurotas. For my sister who had always hated jewels. She was smiling, unaware that he intended to tame her.

But Clytemnestra won't let herself be tamed, I thought, almost prayed, as I sat at that over-long table; she'll never let herself be extinguished. She will burst into flame, Clytemnestra will. She will tear other people to pieces. That's her nature; she can't help it. I was formulating prophecies about the happy bride facing me. I knew her character, but I didn't know my own. If I looked into myself, all I saw was pools of water. They reflected the sun, but there was more to them than that. At least, I thought there was. I've always had some understanding of myself, and I did even then. Perhaps then more than ever. I got up and left the rowdy banquet. I'm made of stone.

3

I went out into the darkness, among the low branches of the olive grove. I walked right round the palace, where the doors had all been left open and everyone, even the humblest slave, had a chance to enjoy a little relaxation and some good food. The lazy rays of the moon gradually grew longer across the polished stone floors. The throne room, through which the breeze was murmuring soft songs, seemed abandoned. I climbed the steps to the throne and placed my hand on its stone seat. A seat like many others, perhaps less comfortable than most. The empty vessel of a useless power. I hurried back down the steps, suddenly afraid because I was alone. Yet the idea of going back through the garden to my place at that long table sickened me. They had bought my sister for a mass of gold and were taking her away. Just as they would have done if it had been me. No, I refused to smile to please them.

I left the palace and headed for the stables. The horses, left by themselves, were whickering peacefully in the jasmine-scented gloom, their eyes black pearls in the darkness. I lifted my clothes to keep them clear of the dirty straw and held out my hand as I approached the wooden bars of the enclosure that contained an elegant white horse with a long muzzle: Leda's mare. The mare let me stroke her muzzle, and dilated her nostrils. Her nose was wet, and I could just see the pink skin under her white coat. Her breath warmed my bare flesh. Then, suddenly alarmed, she shook her head. I listened, and heard hooves speeding towards the stables. Theseus, shouted a terrified voice in my head; there was nowhere, absolutely nowhere I could hide. With no thought for my beautiful white dress I knelt in the straw and crept under the bars of the enclosure between the mare's feet, causing her to neigh in alarm. Better crushed by her hooves than in the power of Theseus, I thought. Much better. I crept into the darkest corner and hid under the heaped-up hay, waiting with my hands over my head, my skin burning hot and the blood crying out in my veins.

The galloping horse stopped in front of the main gate. Someone dismounted with a soft thud. A heavy man. I could hear a jingle of harness. But the tender voice that calmed the animal was not that of Theseus. I cautiously moved on my knees to the wooden bars and peered out. In the white moonlight I could see a horse and rider. When the man tied up his steed by the bridle at the entrance to the stall, I recognized him as the guard who had given me a drink. Unaware of my presence, he took off his sweat-soaked tunic. The horse had already bent his neck to the stone trough, where the man filled a pail with water for himself. He took a long drink, his neck swelling in the moonlight, streams of water running down. The tensed muscles of his shoulders and arms made him look like a god. Afraid he would see me, I moved back out of sight. My mother's mare took fright and neighed again. I crawled between her feet, held my breath and huddled on the ground.

'Who's there?' The soldier's voice. His steps came nearer. 'What's going on?' I was aware of his hand caressing the mare's muzzle, just as I had done myself. Then silence. I lifted my eyes from the straw and met his.

'Who are you? Come out from there.' In the darkness he hadn't recognized me. But there was no sense in staying where I was. I got up with difficulty, not even trying to shake off the dirt. He gave me a puzzled look and opened the wooden door of the enclosure. I came out with my head high, summoning up the little dignity available to a young girl wearing clothes filthy with dung.

'I was afraid,' I said quietly.

'I'll take you back to the palace, princess.' A firm voice, almost as if giving a command. Outside the stable he put on his sweaty tunic again and waited patiently for me in the open space bathed in moonlight, then together we covered the short distance to the back yard of the palace. 'Shall I come with you to your rooms?'

I shook my head. 'I'm fine.'

He looked me in the eyes. 'The Athenian won't come back.'

'But he won't go away either,' I answered in a small voice.

He said nothing more. There was nothing more he could have said. You can't comfort princesses of the blood when you're just an ordinary soldier. He had been dismissed, and turned and went into the barracks.

4

The winter after Clytemnestra left was the longest and coldest anyone could remember. The water froze in the horse troughs and ducks no longer swam on the Eurotas, transformed by ice into a white mirror. A fierce wind swept Sparta for forty days, and with it came a black fever that brought death into every house. Castor was the first to fall ill, one morning after drinking too much, and he died within three days without ever recovering from his delirium. I remember the eyes of Pollux when they told him the terrible news; I saw real grief on his face for the first time. They had only ever loved each other, my brothers, so the bond that held them together had been total. 'A part of me,' murmured Pollux, 'a part of me.' Then he left the room where my mother had already started to tear her hair in accordance with convention. Some hours later, they found him hanged in his room. I never saw his body. They had shut me up in my apartments to protect me from contagion. Only Etra came, bringing me food and water, and even she was under strict orders from my father not to come too close. In the dead of night I would slip through the windows into the icy garden where no one walked any more. I had no fear of the fever. By now I was sleeping free of dreams. Theseus had faded in the boredom of week after week of sameness, faded like my brothers for whom I could not bring myself to weep, and like my parents of whom I heard nothing for some time.

I didn't fall ill. The guard continued to change regularly outside my barred door. I would lean my head against it, trying to distinguish any noise or voice that might help me to understand who was there. For me, only one face had not faded in those days of wind and cold, the only one I wanted to see again. I would come in secretly from the garden by unusual routes. Slipping silently through the shadows, down corridors left deserted by other women, each shut in her own room, I spied on the comings and goings of the sentries. Till finally one night at the changing of the guard a step I remembered well came marching from the far end of the corridor. With my heart drumming in my chest, I waited for the relieved sentry to go after exchanging a few unimportant words with his comrade. Then I emerged nervously from the shadows and approached him.

'Soldier,' I murmured, hoping not to frighten him. He grabbed his spear, as I expected, but recognized me in the dim torchlight.

'Princess! You . . .'

'Shh! I couldn't stay shut up any longer! I . . .'

He watched me from under his helm. Waiting for orders, perhaps. My courage failed. My heart was beating so loudly in my chest that he must have been able to hear it. But outwardly I was just a capricious child, defying the fever and my father's orders to stay in my room. Yet I could not bring myself to command him to open the door for me and not tell anyone of my disobedience. I took a step forward. 'I'm scared,' I admitted and it was true, in that corridor full of great long shadows and silence steeped in other people's panic from behind barred doors. He took off his helm and placed it on the floor beside his spear. Then he knelt down so he could look me in the eyes. He was so much taller than me.

'Princess . . .'

Without thinking, I knelt down too and before my nerve could fail me, took his face in my hands. What did the first humans to create an organized society do? How could they ever have believed they would be able to control their own blood? I examined his face in the flickering torchlight, stroking his hollowed cheeks and fair hair. And looking into those dark green eyes that I would nevermore forget.

'Princess . . .' he said again, very quietly.

'Not princess,' I said as softly as I could, 'Helen . . .' One day I would hate my own name. But on this night it carried within it everything that was me.

'Helen . . .' he almost whispered, his hands at my back to help me to my feet. 'Helen . . .' Without looking at me, he lifted the bar and opened the door. And without looking at him, I crossed the threshold into my room. For a moment his big hand met mine again in the muffled darkness beyond the door. When I turned he was no more than a black silhouette against the red torchlight. Only his eyes were still shining when he disappeared beyond the barrier.

The epidemic lasted another fifteen days. On the sixteenth, Etra came to set me free and held me in a long embrace. 'My child, my child,' she murmured.

'Are many dead?' I asked, pushing her away.

She shook her head. 'Your brothers . . .'

'Are many dead?' I repeated more loudly.

She stroked my face. 'Don't think about it. All cremated and buried already.' I brushed her hand away. She struggled to her feet with a sigh. 'You loved your brothers so much, it's understandable. Their funeral is today. Naturally, because of their rank, they had to come last.' As she talked she picked up a comb, to get me ready.

But I was no longer listening. I was staring in the bronze mirror at a face I did not recognize.

They cremated my brothers together on a single pyre that afternoon. Everyone still left of the Spartan court was there. Both my parents had survived the sickness. My mother, in mourning, had not cut her hair, and hid her lack of tears behind a thick purple veil. The entire corps of the royal guard rattled their spears and shields in salute to the princes as they disappeared in the smoke. Ignored and swaddled like a black dog in my mourning clothes, I looked through the ranks for him. He wasn't there. When the pyre had burnt down and my father asked Etra where I was, she didn't know. She found me much later, wrapped in my cloak in the lowest fork of an olive tree. It took her a long time to persuade me to hand over the scissors I had clenched in my hand. And it took her longer still to collect the long locks of hair I had cut off close to my scalp, and which the wind had entangled with the olive twigs. It was four days before I ate again. All I remember of that period is a void in which no sound reached me. I never knew the soldier's name, and never would know it.

5

In the time that followed I lived in a void, in a state of deprivation. A void that those eyes now lost and burnt had cut into my own. I was myself arid and burnt. Nothing but dull ashes under the skin. But when others looked at me all they saw was a silly child.

The heirs to the throne were dead and Tyndareus was growing old. I took care always to dress, obstinately, in black. Keeping my hair short so it would never grow long again. Fasting to hollow my face and sharpen my cheekbones, rejecting a beauty I could not see, but which refused to disappear in the eyes of others. I was just Helen, nothing more. Nails grown into talons, skin stretched over the bones protruding from my pelvis. Secretly I hoped I would look in the mirror one day and see nothing at all. Leda wasn't interested. I too had learned to close my eyes to the coming and going of officers to her room. It meant nothing to me. I sank daily deeper into a darkness and emptiness that tasted like glue. Down, down, down. To the bottom. I burned my musical instruments. And my light-coloured clothes. There was no beginning or ending to my mourning. Etra watched the burning, and no longer knew what to say. My father wore mourning for two winters; we saw one another from afar in empty corridors; two winters during which I never spoke and never asked anyone for anything. I had become the terror of the palace. Silly maids whispered that I never slept. That I was wandering about the palace looking for the spirits of my dead brothers. They understood nothing. I went back to my rooms where in winter I extinguished the braziers. I plunged into dreams in which he appeared as a distant silhouette against a bright light. Offering me his hand as he did that day in the courtyard; I would go forward to him with arms outstretched but I could never see his face. Sometimes I dreamed of the stuff of his cloak the time he brought me home; the smell and taste of the rough fibre sharp and clear to my nose and tongue. I could see the blond down on his hands and could feel him smiling above me. But I could never capture his green eyes. Those were my worst dreams. I would wake with an unsatisfied need for more sleep. Like a drug. It was then that I began burning laurel leaves. The oracles were said to use them when making prophecies. They were said to open a door to new worlds. I breathed in the thick suffocating smoke, my eyes wide open to the night. But the laurel smoke brought Theseus into my room. There was no longer any guard outside my door. When the smoke at last overcame me, I would collapse in a sleep as dreamless as death. One day Etra found me prostrate beside the brazier. She shook me again and again and called me, but I would not open my eyes. Her voice reached me from far away, as if I were under water. The laurel stood between us, between me and the world. She dragged me into the garden and poured cold water on my head. I woke blinking in a dazzling light, mumbling disconnected words without knowing where I was. Etra beside me was just an indistinct shape.

'Poison. Poison! Never again, child, never again.' Strong arms lifted me. Too slender to have been his. It could have been a promise. Or a threat. Never again, Etra. Never again.

'You must stop cutting your hair. You must start eating again. You could be so beautiful. They'll have to pay a huge sum of gold for you.' Tyndareus was speaking in the neutral tones of a merchant advertising goods in the market. He was sitting by my bed but not looking at me.

There was a sad grey light from the window and the sound of the Eurotas softly singing.

'At first you'll suffer and crave the laurel, but that will pass. You can be sure I shan't let them give you poppy milk, so there won't be any point in asking for it. You'll have to pull through on your own.' He hesitated, as if thinking.

I rested my head on the pillow and looked at him. His eyes shifted away from mine: 'I shall be gone, Helen. Soon I shall be gone. Sparta will need a king. And you will need a husband.'

I didn't answer. I had been out of reach of his demands for a long time already.

'They were my sons too,' he said, talking to himself, his voice breaking into a thousand tiny pieces. But he would not weep, I knew that. Like me, he was made of stone. He looked at me, his eyes searching mine, but they found nothing. I would have liked to shout at him that my eyes were sealed, and that for me everything had been dark since the day of the pyre. But there would have been no point. It would have been useless. He would not have understood. The memory would have to rot down and die inside me, because inside that memory I was strong. No one could reach me. Even if they forced me to marry, I would not resist. I was already safe.

*

It took many months for me to learn to live without the laurel and the visions it had brought me. They uprooted all the hedges in the garden. I developed deep hollows under my eyes, and was afflicted for many days by trembling as if I had been raped. I shouted for a brazier and my leaves. My gateway to a world of nightmares even stronger than my own. Tyndareus ignored me and Leda kept away until I was better. After a month of force-feeding (Etra and two powerful maids crushed my food to pap to stop me choking and prevent me vomiting it back up), I recovered an appearance of sanity, at least so the slave women said. They cut my nails, and my hair started growing again like a thick thatch of flax.

Then Leda came to my rooms wrapped in purple, her neck heavy with gold chains set with pearls, her fair hair beginning to be streaked with grey. She sat down by me as if she had only left me that morning, smiled for a long time and raised a hand to stroke my face. I didn't resist but kept quite still.

The rumour went that she had aborted a courtier's child. I studied her stomach which still looked flat under the folds of her dress. Leda, Leda, what have you done to us?

'I've brought you a few things. To make you beautiful again.' She smiled the smile of an accomplice. At a wave of her hand, slave girls brought in caskets and chests full of jewels and precious cloth. Half the treasure of Sparta. A kingdom where most people wore the one tunic all the year round. My eyes lingered a long time on the glittering gold and precious stones and the fine cloth. Leda watched with satisfaction, as if those treasures my soldier would never have been able to see or touch could ever dispel my pain. It was then I realized it could not help me to stay shut up there. That the pain which was my strength could never protect me from such things. That my salvation existed only in my own sick dreams. I looked at Leda.

'When I'm married will you two go into exile?'

I reached for the nearest casket. Gold and pearls.

Leda had stopped smiling.

6

The summer was half over when Diomedes came. Tyndareus had sent heralds far and wide to announce that he was offering his daughter in marriage, and with her the kingdom of Sparta. But for many months no suitor presented himself and the sumptuous guestrooms stayed empty. 'No one wants our kingdom,' said Leda angrily. She had realized what exile was going to mean for her. A rock in the middle of the Ionian sea. Stones and goats, and no more officers of the guard.

I'm of no interest to anyone, I told myself, smiling at my increasingly healthy reflection in the mirror. I had a familiar ghost walking beside me and needed nothing more. Tyndareus, waiting impatiently for my unknown future husband, stared at me in silence, gloomy reproof in his eyes. I returned his gaze and shrugged my shoulders. The madwoman, they called me in all the courts of Greece, the madwoman. My never-ending mourning had created a scandal. Whispers connected my name with the most atrocious word of all: incest. *She wears mourning for her brothers as one would for lovers* . . .

The thaw came, and after the third winter since the pyre, colours began to bloom again among the stones of Sparta. Emerald-tinted insects danced, and gold flickered in the mild air. But still no messenger, no suitor at the city gates. I began to think this was how we would live for ever, in that palace that was full of folk but always seemed empty. With that sad king, his extinguished flame leaving just ashes. We were enclosed in mourning: Tyndareus, Leda and I.

I learned much later that it was now that Agamemnon sent his first messengers. He made his offer sound like a threat. *My brother Menelaus is looking for a wife and a kingdom. If no suitor comes, Sparta will be mine.*

Tyndareus controlled his temper. He said nothing to me, just forced himself to wait. Then, one evening in high summer, a troop of horsemen crossed the border into Sparta.

The garden was my refuge at night. The slaves who should have been my attendants and companions were afraid of the dark. When the shadows lengthened they would rush with shrill screams into the house, back to their spindles and looms and their pointless gossip. To their clothes and copper finery. But I would stay out of doors, in the fading violet-tinged light. Slipping barefoot along pathways cut in the dry grass. Rocking myself slowly on swings hanging from the low olive branches. By now all my black clothes had been burnt.

That evening the setting sun made the blue of my tunic a dirty grey. With my back to the palace, I sat down on the splintery seat of my favourite swing. I could imagine, beyond the gnarled tree trunks before me, the mud and stone banks of the Eurotas. The cries of soldiers changing guard reached me on the light wind. Apart from this and the almost inaudible sound of running water, the world was silent. Gripping the thick ropes of the swing, I looked out at the emptiness. Letting the light of that unforgotten moonlit night flow into me once more. That evening the light had been like dense rivulets of water running down his lovely body, now petrified for ever by death. My eyes had stolen that beauty, snatching it from the rule of time and sickness. *I shall keep him to myself.* The illusion of an eternity more durable than fire or stone. He could have lived for ever in that light. Confused, I asked myself whether in the emptiness beyond death, spirits could still remember. And if they did remember, could they come back to walk invisible on the earth. I closed my eyes. The wind flecked the leaves like an answer. The springy branches of the olive tree stroked my shoulders. Like his rough palm between my shoulder blades. That touch banished for all time by a cruel Fate. I opened my eyes. The sun had disappeared behind the mountains, only an indistinct crown of fire still lay on the horizon. The stars were searching out their ancient eternal pattern in the sky. The hand of my ghost was still caressing my shoulders in a way not even renewed contact with reality could dispel. But when I turned, I saw a man who was not a ghost studying me without smiling, sitting on the grass.

He had black eyes, or at least they seemed black to me in the deepening night. His furrowed brow was half hidden by unruly dark locks. He had the olive skin of a Greek from the coast. Fine fleshy lips, a strong nose. He had leant forward so he could look me in the eyes. The arms resting carelessly on his thighs were robust and muscular, with large hands. A long white scar stretched in an irregular line over his dark skin from wrist to elbow. Without getting up, I sank my eyes into his like weapons. He held my gaze. Who are you? I wanted to ask. How did you dare to touch me? But such questions would have been pointless in that still evening air. I had long given up caring what others thought, so I bit my tongue and kept silent. I accepted the strange immobility of the slowly descending night with a kind of indifference. Then, unexpectedly, the man stood up and held out his hand. It was only then I noticed how young he was, perhaps only four or five years older than I was. He was wearing a sober sandy tunic. Wrapped round his right wrist was a white ribbon which, when he placed it on his dark curls, revealed itself as a diadem. Greek kings didn't need crowns. I went on looking at him, my head still turned. After a moment of what must have been hesitation even if his features did not betray it, he walked round the olive tree with long measured steps and came face to face with me. I had been following his movements with my head; so the brief moment when he vanished from sight provoked in me a shudder of dismay. Now, facing me, he stood motionless for a moment, then knelt down with a natural movement; close, very close to where I was still sitting on the swing's splintery seat. I lifted my heels from the ground and pulled myself further back, arching my feet, and for a moment they nearly brushed his knees. He continued to watch me with his penetrating gaze, showing no deference whatever, but also no greed or desire. Only a quiet curiosity; perhaps even less than that, a vague serene uncertainty; a wish to understand the strange animal in front of him.

Then with a sudden though unhurried movement he reached for my feet which had been trying to avoid him. Rough palms with thick, hardened skin grasped my ankles, and with a shiver my skin remembered knowing that touch before.

Without warning I got up slowly. I had no thought in my head when I placed my hands on his shoulders. His skin was warm and dry to my touch. I let my fingers run over his throat and neck and through his hair. He continued to look at me. He had slanting eyes and hollow cheeks, and eyebrows that nearly met over his nose. My fingers passed through his dark hair and over his temples and moulded themselves to his sharp cheekbone. Then he lowered his eyes for the first time, resting his head gently against my hand like a tired traveller finding rest. He half closed his lips, then tensed them, while silence spread its petals between us. Imperceptibly my body yielded and fell against his; I huddled against his thighs and chest. My hand never left his cheek, but his arms closed round me and his head bent over mine. His breath on my neck was a tiny breeze.

'Helen,' he murmured, a low voice calling me from deep in his throat.

My name. His voice. Darkness surrounded us like a protective cloak.

The voices of slaves and courtiers filtered through the

olives from the palace; they were preparing dinner, certainly a banquet. Chords were struck from lyres as musicians warmed up; hurrying guards tramped to the main entrances. Etra was perhaps already searching the corridors for me. I slowly unwound my arms and legs from his. After his warmth the grass was cold to my feet. Not wanting to let go of me, his hands followed my movements, and when I got up he did the same.

I lightly touched the firm outline of his jaw, a face my hand already knew by heart. He took my hand and squeezed it. 'Diomedes . . .' I heard his voice murmur.

'Diomedes, Diomedes,' I repeated unsurprised, as if recognizing something I had already known for a long time.

Finally my feet decided to move towards the palace. His hand closed round my wrist and I turned towards him. His eyes were like sparks in the black night and his lips half open. I smiled. My wrist slipped from his compliant hand, and the resignation of the breath escaping from his lips coloured the darkness. I caressed his palm, again laced my fingers with his and squeezed them. I could not see him any more, but could feel him. Together we walked back up the path, towards the pool of golden light from the open windows of the palace.

7

That evening's banquet only lives in my memory as the soft reflections of torches in the eyes of Diomedes. I ate little, not from despair but from pure, simple distraction; my eyes wandering in search of his, constantly finding him over the various dishes and cups, and the vague chatter of the guests. He was of course sitting on my father's right, and Tyndareus every so often looked slowly from him to me, calculating. But the evening meant nothing to me; what transported me was the marvel of hot blood exploding in rapid waves through my veins, the roar of the sea in my ears, the laughter forever frozen in my throat. Because when I found his eyes, my voice died. Eyes that instantly made me forget those other eyes cremated on the pyres. But I felt no shame, because I had neither past nor future, no black hole from which I must laboriously drag myself with nails and teeth, no unlit abyss that might swallow up my days in silence. The man was before me, and that was all. Everyone else was drinking deeply at this banquet given by the king for the first suitor to arrive; Diomedes alone touched no wine. I watched his fingers fiddling idly on the table with the short thick stem of his cup, caressing its contours like the body of a lover, as if studying what was familiar in the moment before he discovered it anew. But then I saw his fingers hesitate on the chiselled rim, never finally closing round the cold goblet of Phoenician glass, never lifting it to his lips. His fingers; I preferred looking at them to studying his face which was marked by heavy, menacing shadows in the candlelight. But to me he was beautiful, beautiful with a ferocious beauty I prayed time would never be able to mar.

I could not have said how long the banquet lasted or how it ended, though I know for certain that my father as usual raised a glass to the gods, rendering grateful thanks as was his duty. Yet I paid no attention to him, conscious only of the dark arm of Diomedes pouring on the floor the last drops of wine from his cup as a final offering to the gods. Then they called me away; Leda using her vague, melodious voice to rip apart the veil of my self-satisfaction. I smiled, with the lost smile of a laurel addict. I saw my mother frown; pulling her carefully drawn brows together and wrinkling her perfect forehead like parchment. Her manicured hand closed brutally on my arm, demanding an explanation, but over her shoulder I could see Diomedes watching me from the door. When she saw his eyes fixed on us, she completely relaxed her harpy's scowl and the grip on my arm, quickly letting her hand slip down with maternal complicity to grasp my palm. And then, apparently smiling at no one at all but actually at Diomedes, she took me away.

When we reached my room Leda set her favourite woman slave on guard at the door. She took my hand and made me sit down on the bed, chattering confusedly in her excitement, unable to keep still: 'The first one ... mad about you ...'

Mad about you. I could see myself in the mirror behind her shoulder, and allowed myself a spontaneous smile. Diomedes mad about me! For the first time I was sorry I hadn't let my hair grow back. Its present bristles were an odd frame for my face. I was nothing like the girl Theseus had carried off, or even the girl who had inhaled the powerful laurel smoke. Who was I, then? No doubt I would find out, but the bronze mirror was reflecting unformed clay, with no definite shape yet. My mother was watching me with knowing eyes, concentrating hard as she looked from me to the mirror. It was as if she could read my thoughts.

'Let me prepare you. You'll be remarkably beautiful.'

'Prepare me . . . ?'

'Yes. Diomedes will come to find you, you can be sure of that.'

I said nothing more, savouring her words like the wine I hadn't drunk and the food I hadn't eaten. I let her comb my hair to hide the uneven cut, and fetch me a new tunic from her rooms. Then she started on me again, fastening the tunic with gold buckles, and painting my lips carmine and my brows blue and black.

'There! A queen!' As she studied me she bit her lip, only too aware that she was preparing another woman to take her place. But at that moment her future exile didn't matter. What she was seeing in the mirror was another Leda. I asked myself in anguish if Diomedes might have been attracted to her. Naturally, my mother's brilliant smile told me as she got ready to go, who on earth could fail to fall for Leda? What man could ever say no to her? Not Diomedes, for sure. Not a king.

She kissed my cheek before she went. Assuming I would know what we were talking about. But her soft lips tasted dark on my skin. She departed with her usual sparkle, leaving me still searching for her reflection in the mirror.

Not searching for myself, but for her. But the cheekbones I saw were too pronounced and the mouth too wicked for Leda. I wanted to wipe off the make-up at once with the back of my hand. But remembering my king dressed in yellow ochre I decided not to.

I lay down on the bed to wait. Somehow, I don't know how, I was convinced Diomedes would respect no rules. On the other hand, my mother had made clear to me that I could expect him to come and find me. And the thought of this acceptable transgression filled my blood with disgust. I waited. The oil gradually burned down in the lamp. I watched the flame tremble and go out, drowned in a sea of black. Sleep weighed heavy on my eyelids, smoothing down my lashes with gentle fingers. I shook my head with annoyance, but eventually gave in. Then sleep took me in his arms and began playing his strange tricks. As always, I dreamed I was following my lost love through spirals of smoke. But now he was coming towards me and taking my face in his hands with barely controlled violence. Looking straight into my eyes. His own were sharp green silica splinters. He was accusing me. I woke and managed not to cry out; my throat was clamped in iron. He was my love, I had silently sworn that I loved him. And forgotten already. I got off the bed, but my legs were feeble, bloodless and without strength. A gold buckle came loose and fell to the floor with a dull thud. I timidly approached the mirror. And hated what I saw. A whore. Sleep had smudged the make-up round my eyes, turning my face into a grotesque mask. My mouth was a bloody and discontented grimace. Old. It was my mother's face after a night with one of her soldiers. No. I was angry and ripped cloth violently from brooches. The clasps hit the floor with a dull sound, a lament of metal on stone. My fingers ruined Leda's patient construction that she had based on the ancient art of seduction. And Diomedes had not come.

Outside my windows dawn was painting the world in shades of rose. I threw on my blue tunic again. And went out through the window as I had not done since the days of the plague, climbing over the sill and dropping to the ground. I ran barefoot down the slippery compacted earth and felt sun-dried grass sting my ankles. But I also felt a strange, almost mad, urge to laugh and cry out that I was happy. Ask me that now. Whether I'm happy. Running, at least this time. I was like Clytemnestra before she gave up her white tunics. And beside me my ghost, silent still, but placated. His, mine. I had forgotten the previous evening like a drunken binge that had never happened. I heard the Eurotas before I saw it, I heard its sharp, cutting song. A tinkling not of silver but of iron behind the drawn curtains of the trees. Sparta's river could only be a ferocious river. I crossed its pebbled bank and threw myself into its icy waters without even taking off my clothes, the natural continuation of my headlong race from the trees on to the bank, with my arms spread wide so as not to slip. Then I was in the river. All of me, without regret or hesitation. Hands, head, neck, body, legs, feet. The whole of me in that steely embrace. Like plunging a red-hot blade into water to temper it. A brutal embrace grabbed me above and below and all round. Opening my eyes I saw whirlpools of sand and mud and gently undulating weeds like the hair of a drowned man anchored to the bottom just below the surface. A fish flashed silver among the greenery, a red stripe down its back. I reached out to touch it, but it vanished. I came up again, my newly growing hair thrown back like a whiplash and my mouth open, panting for air. Farewell to dreams, farewell to ghosts in that clean bracing early morning air.

It was then that Diomedes came up behind me, so that I did not hear him. He grasped me firmly, pressing my shoulders against his body and pulling me under. The world filled with bursting bubbles as he dragged me down till I touched the river bed. He was strong, stronger than I was. I struggled but I had never been an athlete. I gave in with my nails gripping his arm, waiting for him to pull me up again. When he released me and I could feel fresh air in my lungs, I turned to look at him, my veins streaming with fury. He was smiling. I hit his face, hard. He went on smiling, his legs and arms still moving incessantly against the river. He pushed me out of the current, towards the bank. I wanted to vomit insults, I prayed for my ghost to return as flesh and blood. But Diomedes did not let me speak. With fiercely concentrating eyes and gentle hands he dried my face, removing the last traces of my make-up. His fingers pushed back my hair. 'There.' Shaking him off I got to my feet and sat down on a flat stone lightly lapped by the water. I could feel my tunic glued to my skin, and combed my hair with my fingers. He dragged himself up to me with lazy movements of his arms against the shallow bed of the river, his eyes smouldering like embers in a brazier long after the fire has gone out.

My feet were dangling in the water. Like on the first evening, he took them in his hands. And looked at me. No longer smiling. His mouth curled with doubt and the seed of a distant fear of refusal. I studied the trees. With the green light filtering through their foliage, I could believe in spirits. Was my burnt love watching me there, tall and dark under a white poplar? I should have got up and gone to him. But they say the living cannot walk with the dead. Diomedes squeezed my ankle, forcing me to look down. He rose in the water, his lips tracing a path from my foot to my knee, but stopping firmly there. A shudder not caused by cold water ran from my neck to my legs, stretching skin and nerves, even touching my bones. I looked at the trees again, but lost sight of the green light when the hands of Diomedes closed round my waist. Accepting no refusal, he pulled me into the water and against his body. I sank as he forced me to stretch out on the sloping bed of the river. Stones and mud parted under my back, but I couldn't resist him, letting myself go with my eyes open and my hands locked behind his neck beneath the surface of the water. He let me pull him with me. His eyes were open like mine, too close to me. Then his mouth was on mine, his eyelashes meeting mine in the water. His wound his legs round mine, searching for support. My first kiss. We re-emerged breathless. I backed off without getting up, imperceptibly surrendering, supporting myself on feet and hands. Till I could feel the pebbles under my fingers. Diomedes pursued me, his eyes on mine, advancing as I retreated. Until all I could do was untie the now useless knot of my sodden tunic which his hands were pushing up my thighs as he crushed me under his weight. Over his head was a green and golden light, like glass. As I let myself go I could hear my ghosts turn and go away.

8

It was a day that passed too quickly. No one came into the woods, no one came to look for us. Our bodies dried in the sun, the river washed the bloodstains off the rocks. The court of Sparta forgot about the king of Argos; my mother never sent anyone to look for me. Under the relaxed supervision of our needy kingdom, I was free. Diomedes chased me like a child and took me, pressing me against the grass. The whole of my being was in his kisses and in his hands. I laughed, that day. I had forgotten the music of my laughter, which bounced like stones off a wall. He said he loved me, which made me laugh even more because I knew it was a lie. He took me by the waist and lifted me high in the air. Then let himself fall with me on the harsh grass of the meadow. He was breathing as easily as lifting a piece of cloth.

He turned towards me with his eyes shining. 'Marry me, Helen.'

I laughed again; but in his black irises lit by the sun with gilded gleams there was an anxiety I had not expected. I thought of my burnt love, but he was not there under that gentle sun. I did not answer Diomedes but laughed again, and he understood. On that meadow he pushed up my blue tunic again. I did not stop him. My breath merged with the buzzing of the bees settling among the wild flowers.

We walked hand in hand back to the palace. The sun had struggled up the sky until midday, then slowly slipped down till it vanished with its halo behind the blue and black mountains. We watched the sunset lying on thick grass surrounded by sheep. Some shepherds who did not know who we were offered us black bread and hard cheese. It was lovely to watch Diomedes talking with those old men gnarled like olive trees, and biting with hesitant teeth into the impenetrable crust of their humble bread. I crowned a lamb with a brushwood garland. It stumbled over its own thin legs trying to reach the dangling twigs with its toothless mouth. And when the long shadow of the Peloponnese tinted the sheep's woollen coats with violet and dogs ran about rounding up the animals with wolfish barks, Diomedes pressed his lips against my neck and offered me his hand to lead me away.

'Wait,' I said. A last hazy crown of red fire was still for a moment framing the jagged silhouette of the mountains before it vanished completely. The sheep were gone. Slender wisps of smoke from the cooking of humble suppers climbed from distant hovels in the valley. All was silent and deserted. Only that sparse, hesitant smoke told us we were not the last survivors on the face of the earth. I began to get up.

He was so much taller than me. To help me to my feet he needed to bend like a willow in a storm.

We decided to walk hand in hand to the palace, and ask my father for a consent I did not think we would need.

The sentries at the gate came to attention in a formal salute, ignoring our tousled hair and disordered clothes. There were fragments of hay in Diomedes' black locks like precocious strands of grey. I smiled and gently brushed them away.

The king's chief counsellor came to meet us: 'King of Argos, we have been waiting for you.' Diomedes sighed. He had kept his white fillet round his wrist all day. Now he abruptly unwrapped it.

I stood on tiptoe to arrange it on his dark curls while he bowed his head as if I were crowning him. The smile never left his lips. He squeezed my hand: 'I will see you later.'

Then for a brief instant, before all hopes were dashed, I felt certain he and I would grow old together, and die together, in a palace not much different from this one. The thread of my life would be woven and cut together with his. I did not realize Leda was behind me until I heard her gracious tones. I turned. She was old, and wrinkles seemed to have appeared at the corners of her eyes in a single evening.

'I'm happy for you,' she murmured in a tired voice.

I considered her, looking into her lovely blue eyes; she had denied me that refuge as a child, but now I dived in, on this evening when the air consisted of glass too thick to allow the passage of any lies. I said nothing, but took a step forward and embraced her. At first she stood as rigid as wood, but gradually let herself go. I could feel her soft skin against my body, the folds of her dress, the great gold brooches that held her clothes together. Her skin was fragrant with rose. Then she let go of me, stroked my face for a brief moment, and went away. I did not wait to watch her disappear at the far end of the corridor.

9

Diomedes started back for Argos the following morning, with a promise from my father and his consent to our marriage. He left on horseback, his regal fillet wrapped as always round his strong dark wrist. My parents stood stiffly at the top of the steps. My mother had already stooped smiling. I shuddered as I remembered how Castor and Pollux had seen Theseus off from the same place when he left with me wrapped in his cloak. I ran down the steps. The horses were pawing the ground, held back with difficulty by their riders. The men of the escort smiled when Diomedes, already in his saddle, grabbed me by the waist, pulled me up and placed me in front of himself on his horse's back. He gave me a long passionate kiss as if no one else were there. As always he gazed into my eyes while he stroked my hair; his eyes laughing: 'What's wrong, Helen? I'll be back in no time, then you'll have all the time in the world to get tired of me.'

'That can never be too soon,' I answered, but so quietly he didn't hear. He put me down on the ground. Then at a signal from Diomedes his escort set off at a gallop. He raised his arm in farewell. His horse reared up and back down, and without stopping passed through the court-yard gate. Soon the group were just clouds of dust on the road among the hills. When I turned back, the king and queen of Sparta had already gone. I went back into the house alone.

So began a time of perfect happiness for me. Merchants were called in to help with my trousseau; Egyptian and Cretan goldsmiths for the jewellery. I was sure Diomedes would raise no objections. Chests full of costly brilliance, with my father seeming calmer now as he realized that Sparta would have a young king. A warrior king. Leda had stopped entertaining officers in her rooms. She was already beginning to say farewell. It was then and only then, with vagabonds and merchants carrying the length and breadth of Greece the news that Diomedes the Brave, Diomedes son of Tydeus and King of Argos, had asked for and been granted the hand of the mad Helen; it was only then that others began to take an interest. The dust of Sparta whitened the boots of one after another as they came to ask for my hand in marriage from my father. I never met these suitors who came and went. No banquet was ever given in their honour; they were sent on their way with cold courtesy. Tyndareus had no feeling for any of them except Peleus. Peleus and his son Achilles.

I did not know they had come, and never had any reason to expect them to come, that they would travel the long road all the way from Phthia. But one day I was in my garden when a man I did not know walked through the trees: Achilles, who was as young as myself, perhaps too young. They said of him as they said of me, that he was mad.

He walked calmly through the olive trees and sat down at my side. 'They want us to get married,' he said, as though it was obvious, as though we had already been discussing the subject a few moments before.

I shrugged. 'I'm marrying someone else.'

He didn't stop smiling. 'I know. But my father's an obstinate man.'

I did not look up at once, but when I did I saw he had been looking at me.

'You're beautiful, Helen.'

I could not lower my eyes again. Achilles's skin was

honey-gold and his hair just a little darker; his eyes between green and blue. We spent the rest of the afternoon talking together, and did not notice the sun going down. Late that evening, after everyone else had gone to sleep, he came to my window; making sure the lights were out, I opened the shutters and let him in. We made love slowly and silently on my bed, then he lay awake in my arms. It was only with the coming of the rosy morning light of Eos that he slipped away from my side. I watched him dress beside my bed.

'Goodbye, Helen,' he said, smiling with no sadness in his voice, closure achieved. They left at midday and I did not go out to watch them leave.

10

Now even more men were coming from all over Greece in hopes of the throne of Sparta. Horse after horse came into the courtyard. I no longer even bothered to look. But one day Leda came to my rooms, the anguish of catastrophe in her eyes.

'Who is it this time?' I asked in alarm.

'A messenger.'

I put down my distaff and thread, and looked askance at her.

'From Mycenae,' added my mother.

A command from the great king. A command that allowed no refusal. My sister sent greetings and all her love, which stung me like a whiplash. They informed us they would come to Sparta in time for the wedding, but not before. That would give us plenty of time to dispose of Diomedes, King of Argos. Another messenger would already have reached him by now, reported Agamemnon's messenger in a neutral voice between one cup of wine and the next. I expected Diomedes to take three days to reach us, but he did it in a day and a half, arriving on a horse flecked with foam which he forced up the steps to the palace entrance. Galloping through the corridors, he found my father administering justice in the throne room. Tyndareus said nothing but signed to us all to leave, including me. Diomedes never looked at me at all. As if he had already said goodbye. A clean break. And I wept for Achilles and the long road to Phthia that would have taken me so far, too far from Sparta.

'I have to go now, Helen.'

'I know, Diomedes.'

That evening I had the chests containing my trousseau dragged into the garden and burned them.

11

Menelaus was a good man. Watching him come across the throne room towards me, I was sure of that. Good. And in love with me from the moment his eyes first caressed my skin. Menelaus, Menelaus. Agamemnon's voice carried a note of derisory compassion. Good in a pathetic sense, yes. The big brown eyes of an abandoned dog. Lifeless ginger hair. Commonplace features unworthy of a prince of the blood. He must be given Sparta because he could not have Mycenae. He timidly offered me his hand. Tyndareus gave me an icy look; I was in no position to ignore that hand. Pain was the first feeling my husband inspired in me, and I hated both him and myself that it must be like that. Menelaus, with his narrow shoulders and short legs. My hand closed on a sweaty palm.

Clytemnestra was pregnant for the second time. Sitting at her husband's side, her smile as wolfish as ever. But I had enough fire in me now to cope with that. I'm made of stone. I stepped forward and kissed Menelaus on the right cheek.

The banquet was an exact replica of the one held so many years ago for my sister's wedding. The garden lit by torches, the palace empty. And this time I was the one sitting in the middle, dressed for the last time in white. But not shackled by a neckband. Menelaus's present was a long gold-and-pearl necklace. Imperfect, irregular pearls. My fingers fiddled with them as the banquet dragged on, course after course. While outside the tent of torchlight, my silent ghosts began to walk again.

Leda was determined to prepare me for my wedding night. Clytemnestra and Agamemnon were to sleep in the next room. From the flat tone of Leda's voice I understood this to mean they intended to spend the whole night with their ears glued to the wall.

'Menelaus is such a fool he won't know the difference between menstrual blood and a ruptured hymen. Just be careful to keep yourself to yourself tonight. Modesty must be your excuse.'

I nodded in silence. My throat was dry. I had been experiencing a sort of vomitless nausea since I saw Diomedes gallop away.

'Listen, Helen.' Leda's voice was harsh with pain. She was holding my chin with three fingers, forcing me to look her in the eye. 'I never wanted this for you. I'd have spared you from it if I'd been able to.'

I believed her. My voice came from far away. 'I know.'

But she made no attempt to hug me. She knew I was beyond her help. Lost. She unhooked my necklace and laid it on the table: 'Shall I brush your hair for you?'

Yes. Anything to delay the moment of calling in my husband. I sat down in front of the bronze mirror. A wooden comb for untangling knots. The hands of a mother now elderly enough to allow herself to be gentle. The face of a stranger who would never be Helen again. Sold for a pile of gold. No more dreams. Have a good look, learn what to remember. Tomorrow will be different. It's not the sex, Helen. It's this crown that's so heavy. It's this absence that gnaws at you. It's this man you have to share your bed with, that you feel such pity for that you'll end up hating him. That's obvious, Helen. And you'll never sniff laurel again, you've promised that.

But I can't bear another moment of this brutal reality.

Leda put down the comb and tied up my hair with a

ribbon. Then she went away in silence. I went on looking at the bronze reflection in the mirror. Well combed hair and a white tunic. I didn't want to weep, just to cry out, but there would have been no point. Tyndareus and Leda were leaving the next morning. Before it was too late and without looking, I pulled the absorbent bandage away from my thighs. An instant later Menelaus opened the door. A timid squeaking of hinges and silent steps on the floor. I blew out the lamp.

There was a cruel light next morning; it violently forced open my eyes. Turning, I was relieved to find the bed empty. Menelaus had done his duty. When he reached out to take me in his arms I did not move. Not that I could have done anything to stop my blood flowing and giving me away. I'm made of stone. Yes, he pulled me to him and I didn't react, but he must have sensed rejection in my tense muscles. I just didn't want him. I might have been sorry about it. Kind but with silent hatred boiling in my veins. But I couldn't pretend, not about something like that.

With a sigh he had turned away to lie on his back. I pulled the sheet tightly round myself, wanting to weep. But I couldn't, and that hurt me even more. The dry air stung my eyes. Menelaus was soon asleep and snoring, grunting through his short nose, arms invading my side of the bed. Through the wall I could hear Clytemnestra moaning, like the bitch they claimed I was.

Stiff with dried blood and sperm, the sheet scratched my skin. Disgusted, I went to wash myself. Soon a maid came to take the dirty sheet because Agamemnon wanted to inspect it. A couple of confident knocks on my door. I called out come in, combing my hair with furious wrenching strokes. It was Clytemnestra, no less. Already made up at that early hour, with precious stones in her flame-coloured hair.

'Had a good night?'

She was smiling. I pursed my lips, forcing the comb painfully through my hair, and didn't answer. She sat down on the edge of the bed, carefully balancing her big round belly and stroking it with insufferable smugness.

'I'll pretend I heard a yes.'

I felt poisonous. 'Suit yourself, sister.'

She favoured me with an easy, icy smile. 'They're leaving this morning, you know. You'll have to come and say goodbye.'

Tyndareus and Leda. I dropped the comb and hesitated before putting on the pearl necklace, though I knew Menelaus would expect me to wear it. I stood up. Clytemnestra's thin mouth twisted in a grimace of disgust. 'You should look after yourself better.'

'You mean like you? I'm still more beautiful than you are, don't forget.'

She grabbed my wrist. Even with her swollen belly, she was stronger than I was.

'Be very careful, Helen.'

But I wasn't a child, not any longer. Her hatred couldn't reach me any more. I smiled and shook her off. '*Little mums* first,' I said, ceremoniously ushering her to the door. She walked out with dignity, her eyes reduced to slits. I took a last look in the mirror. I did not know the woman I saw. That was what they had achieved. Two deep creases were appearing at the corners of my mouth.

12

Carriages and horses. A king. Agamemnon standing before the main door with his arms crossed, a sumptuous cloak of Phoenician linen round his shoulders. Menelaus at his side with a white royal fillet round his head. Fillets: I remembered Diomedes in the sun in the middle of that courtyard, and now this tiny man. My husband gave me a timid smile, and I smiled back. He wasn't to blame. So long as I could believe that, I could smile for him. Tyndareus was already waiting in a two-seater coach, with his driver holding the horses.

What is the right way to take leave of your father? Should you run down the steps and hug him? Not us. Not me with Tyndareus. I looked down on his wrinkled face from the top step and said goodbye from there. He nodded. That was all.

'It'll take us two days to the sea, Menelaus, then I'll send the horses back. We have a ship waiting to take us to Cephalonia.' The kingdom of their exile: rocks, cliffs and goats. My cousin Penelope and her husband Ulysses lived next door just across the water.

Leda came silently out of the palace behind me. She embraced Clytemnestra, then turned to me. 'Queen of Sparta, I salute you.'

'I'm still Helen, Mother.' A lie, and I knew it.

Leda gently stroked my cheek. 'You have my jewels, daughter. Make the most of them. And sometimes think of me.'

Behind her back, Clytemnestra's already sour expression froze. All I could do was bow my head and accept my mother's words.

Agamemnon and Menelaus bowed too; Leda acknowledged them both with a regal inclination of the head. Then she dropped her bright veil over her face, walked down the steps without a backward glance, and vanished behind the linen curtains of her waiting litter. Tyndareus looked at us one more time. His eyes fixed on the palace of Sparta, his palace, as if he knew Leda must be feeling the same behind the drawn curtains of her litter. He had lived an entire life there. I saw his lips moving, but could not read them. He did not speak, just made a brusque gesture. His driver climbed up and shook the reins. Sharp cries echoed round the courtyard as the cortège moved off. Four slaves lifted my mother's litter and fell in behind the rest. As they did so, a breath of wind moved the linen curtains to reveal for a moment a simply dressed woman, with no jewellery, a sight never seen before even when she was in mourning. It must have been my imagination, I told myself, but I thought I saw tears on her cheeks. Then the curtain fell back and the procession disappeared through the gate. Even Tyndareus had turned away to fix his eyes on the mountains of the Peloponnese. The royal guard drawn up on the road hit their shields with their lances in salute. A war cry ran from house to house through Sparta. Nothing more. Only empty streets under the midday sun.

13

Agamemnon and Clytemnestra stayed the next day and the day after that. Used to taking orders from his older brother, Menelaus was silent and thoughtful, letting the King and Queen of Mycenae give a banquet each evening at the expense of the Spartan treasury. Parties and singing, my sister wearing new jewellery every day, shouts and cries in the night. My own marriage consisted of nothing in the opaque night but the brief panting of Menelaus, who seemed to be quickly tired even by making love. When I dressed I made little effort for him apart from wearing his necklace, and felt happy when my plain unpainted face revealed to my mirror that I was exhausted from lack of sleep.

It irritated me to see my sister dancing, carelessly swinging her stomach and laughing all the time. I could not laugh. Music no longer had any power over me, and my lips were automatically stretched in fixed smiles that deceived no one but Menelaus. Agamemnon bared his teeth and raised a full cup of wine to toast my life, ruined by his actions. The red lips behind his curly black beard were like the leer of a demon from the underworld.

It was only when the queen's belly had grown so heavy that she could hardly walk, that one grey morning Agamemnon gave the order for departure.

'The boy must be born in Mycenae,' he announced, harnessing his carriage. He saw himself as a simple man, did Agamemnon, using no coachman and doing the driving himself.

Clytemnestra, her rapidly swelling figure glittering with gold, was barely capable of leaning forward to say goodbye to me. 'We'll meet again soon, little sister,' she said, displaying her canines with her eyes shining. It took two female slaves to lift her into her litter. Then with a languid gesture she informed her husband that she was ready to start.

'Right you are, my queen,' cried Agamemnon in his deep, kingly voice. A sharp jerk on the reins, and they were off. Standing on the steps, I watched trotting horses raising the dust yet again.

The courtyard was empty. Now the new king of Sparta

could smile, free at last of the shadow of his tiresome brother. But the sky was full of clouds and his queen's face as cold as stone.

I forgot my kingdom, the Sparta of my ancestors beyond the palace walls. It no longer existed as far as I was concerned. But Menelaus was happy; he liked going down into the streets and enjoyed the approval of his people. Little Menelaus, ridiculously small among tall warriors chosen for their fine figures. Yet they learned to respect him, and even became devoted to him. They admired his fairness, his sense of justice. The fact that he was a warrior. All they had known of me was my madness. They had never been my people. They learned to ignore the sad queen who never ventured beyond her garden. I passed my days under the olive trees of my childhood, leaving my spindles and looms on the ground. I had a retinue of slaves who never spoke in loud voices, barely even whispered, and the wind from the Eurotas swept their whispers away. The sound of the river, where I never swam any more, became the backdrop of my boredom. A dull, colourless existence, over before it had even begun. They had stolen my life, leaving no one for me to fight. Helen was dead, twice dead, and it was too late for her to be born again. No prince would climb over the walls. No gods inhabited the altars any longer. And no sun from the sky could penetrate my clouds. I crushed leaves beneath my feet as I walked in blood-red sunsets and danced with my ghosts among the trees. My longing for my soldier came back to dwell in my heart, and I often thought I could see him in the dim light at the end of corridors. I was navigating gently on a slow sea, borne up not by desperation, but by the still death of every hope I had ever nurtured. The swing had been removed from the garden. It was as if Diomedes had never existed.

It was during this uncertain time that Achilles came again.

The slow monotonous succession of unvarying days had engulfed me; boredom thickening my blood and sapping colour from my life. My hair had become loose and dull and I no longer bothered to comb it. But Menelaus noticed nothing. I didn't even have the strength to begin hating him as I had expected to. My husband was just the man who sat on the throne of Sparta administering justice, trained in the stadium with his special guard, and came to my room at night for a few brief moments of rough and tedious pleasure. I ignored him, he was just part of that grey sequence of repeated events into which I had fallen unawares and couldn't be bothered to fight against. In any case, there was nothing left worth fighting against. As those who had shaped my life saw it, all that remained for me now was to bring into the world an heir for the son of Atreus, and when I had achieved that, my life would have no other function. But from the mountains, out of the rising sun, came galloping the men of Phthia.

He came looking for me in the garden just as he had once before, such a long time ago. In that dull world he put Menelaus in the shade and shone like gold. Achilles. I put down my shuttle.

The voice of my husband spoke from behind him. 'What a pleasant surprise, prince. You must be our guest for as long as possible. I know you have met the queen before . . .'

I lifted my eyes to meet his. The same unbearable colour.

'Allow me to show you round Sparta,' Menelaus went on. 'I think I've got used to my kingdom by now, even if there's never enough time; it's rather a special city, of course . . .'

'I'm sure Sparta needs your attention, and I should hate to get in the way of your duties. If the queen is agreeable, I'll just stay in the palace.' The voice of Achilles was calm and peaceful. I never experienced his legendary wrath. But it was a strong voice, not that of a general or a king, but expecting obedience. Menelaus stepped back as if he had been punched. Achilles continued to watch him, as if indifferent to my own response. I kept still, looking at my shuttle lying on the grass.

'If our guest would like to stay,' I said, 'we would be discourteous to deny him.' My voice was flat and my heart beating very softly. I had no idea if it was still able to beat any faster. In the silence that followed I was conscious of the birds singing in the garden.

Menelaus cleared his throat. 'Whatever you like. I'll be back before evening.'

I ignored him as he walked quickly away across the grass. Far off, beyond the gate, the guards beat their lances in salute.

Without looking up I gave a command in a low voice: 'You may leave.' A swish of dresses was enough to tell me that my slave girls had obeyed me, leaving their looms abandoned on the grass like mute traces of a catastrophe that never happened. Achilles sat down beside me, his honey-coloured hands pushing the shuttle out of the way. I looked up. Green flames, Diomedes had once said, flames from the gods of the underworld. The flames that now came from the eyes of Achilles were hard and compact, in colour somewhere between blue and grey. Like a wall. As if they were searching for an answer to I knew not what question.

'You seem exhausted.'

'I know.'

'But you're still the loveliest woman in the world.'

'No one cares about that any more. Certainly I don't.'

'But I do.' He took my hand. I looked at my fingers, thin and pale against his rough palm. Weather-beaten by the sun and wind of his distant island. I did not close my fingers.

'I'm about to go away. My father wants me to go to Scyros, to his friend Lycomedes. To finish my education, he says. But the fact is he's ashamed of me. He thinks I'm mad.' He closed his eyes, as if waiting. As if giving me a chance to agree or disagree. Either to say nothing, or to say yes, King Peleus was right.

'That's what they say about me too.'

He smiled. 'That's why I am the one who should have married you, Helen of Sparta. Just say the word and I'll take you away even now.'

I looked down. 'Menelaus doesn't deserve that.'

He laughed. 'No, it's *you* who don't want it, Helen. You'd rather fade away lamenting for what they've taken from you.'

I felt my eyes grow hard. 'Is it wrong for me to mourn for my life?'

'Don't let them destroy you.' His eyes were stronger than mine, and he lifted my chin to force me to look at him. 'You're too beautiful to fade away.'

I pushed his hand away. 'I'm just property, nothing but merchandise for your pleasure. If only I could just be an ordinary woman . . .'

'I'd have come looking for you even if I'd known you were dressed in rags. Even if you were a hundred years old. Your spirit is what I need, Helen, and I can see that a spark of it still exists. Your beauty would be meaningless to me without that spark. That's why I'm here today. For that brilliant gleam I've known in no other woman.'

I looked up. 'I'm made of stone.'

He smiled. 'Which is how I know you'll never let that fire go out.'

I let his words enter me, gradually dispersing my fatigue. A spirit of fire. To my surprise he picked up the shuttle and rewound the thread.

'Come on, queen, get on with your work, and while you're working you can talk to me. Tell me what happened after I left.'

I took the shuttle from him and leaned it against the loom: 'I went to bed early, Achilles. There's not much to say.'

'Never mind. I'll listen just the same.'

14

Menelaus didn't come home that evening. He sent a herald to tell me he was going to sleep in the barracks with his soldiers. And that I must look after our guest. The counsellors saw me receive the herald and looked at me for news. There was no hypocrisy or corruption at the court of Sparta. My father Tyndareus had taken care of that. The counsellors waited confidently so they could assess me against the sharp edge of their bitter experience. There had to be something missing in their mad queen, the incestuous, the deceiver.

Achilles was standing at my side, motionless in the bright sunlight of day that sharply divided him into light and shadow. There was something lacking in the son of Peleus, he was mad, wild and a deceiver.

'We'll give a banquet,' I announced in the silence.

The counsellors shook their heads. Spartans. Achilles smiled.

The opaque sky tore itself open in a sunset of fire. Achilles watched, standing under the olives. I slithered down the loose hillside to join him, silver bracelets tinkling on my wrist. He never even turned, but I knew he was smiling.

'I can hear the tinkle of jewellery, Helen of Sparta.'

'You hear well, Achilles of Phthia,' I smiled back, imagining the sun playing on the stones in my comb; for the first time in ages, for far too long, I was ready to be admired. But when he did look round no smile brightened his dark face.

'Achilles of nowhere. And, my queen, I'm afraid they're coming for you.' I turned. A slave girl was slithering awkwardly down the path I had just taken, her white dress tinted pink by the light. Before I could answer, Achilles walked away with his back to the sun. Wait, I wanted to say, but the word stuck in my throat. He was moving so quickly I had no chance of catching up with him. Marked with impatience and a dark shadow of heavy premonition in the triumphant light of the dying day. A light made bloody by glory.

The sunset was silently fading into black velvety night when I poured a libation to the gods to start the banquet.

I was wearing my white diadem, and ranged round the table as if sculpted in stone were the grey wolves of my father's council, his tacit tribute to the weakness of my husband. I could almost hear them snarling: look at this woman daring to raise a cup to the gods; Helen's just like Leda, and after this nothing would surprise them. I grasped the black cup by its two handles and lifted it to my lips. The last drops must be poured on the ground for the gods. Let their mute will be done.

The banquet started. Against a sound like the dismal humming of furious bees, a heavy pall of mistrust. A suitor returned. An absent king leaving his queen on the loose. They were curling their lips in scorn, I could see that. Menippus, who had been captain of the guard for more years than I could remember, was assessing Achilles with a look previously reserved for my mother's lovers. And beneath the contempt in his eyes was an indefinable fear. They said Achilles had grown up among monsters and had devoured lions, and Menippus was an old man who believed the stories he heard. But his fear meant nothing to me. Nor did their fear and contempt mean anything to Achilles. I dimly remembered Diomedes under those same lights, but it was a faded memory from long ago. The dissolving mist of an unreal past, meaningless on an evening like this. Achilles saw me watching him, and meeting my eye, slowly tilted his cup over the edge of the table. Drop followed drop to the floor. Honouring a promise. Menippus watched and knitted his brows. But I was the only one who understood. I smiled in the pink light; I had already poured my own offering to the dark god.

When I reached my room, Achilles was already there. Sitting by the window, half lit by moonlight. Sitting by the window, sharply divided into light and shadow. I stood for too long, motionless in the doorway, watching him, assessing the strange harmony of his face. I could hear the muffled hammering of my heart deep inside me. Then I rushed to him with futile joy, my hand held out as though terrified he would vanish from under my very fingers. He said nothing but his hands opened like rough flowers on my arms and hips and round my waist. The night belonged to me, in no sense a concession or a gift. And a second farewell, one I could never have hoped for. He was on me and inside me, and my heart melted no less than my limbs as I fell backwards.

It was sweet to feel his weight on top of me afterwards. His head, and our four arms. We had no need of words. We just needed the moonlight pouring on our two bodies, and the peace. We were like ivy in sunlight shamelessly winding itself round branches, his hair on my mouth, his head on my heart.

'I shall die young.'

'You'll never die.'

'By the sword. Not in bed. Uncomforted. Biting the dust.'

'That seems a bad way to die.'

'Those gods I don't believe in swear in their oracles that sparks of glory will be mixed with the dust.'

'What do you believe in, Achilles?'

'In this present moment burning through time without ever being able to return. In your warmth caught here and now in my hand. In this life living long after our lives are over.'

'I shall die alone.'

'Two bad deaths, then, Helen of Sparta. It would be better to make an end now.'

'In this eternal moment.'

'But leaving us behind.' His eyes searched for mine. Those eyes whose black pupils shone from within irises dulled by the light. We waited together for the dawn. It was only at first light that sleep wrapped us in its gentle shadow. But in that night and in that light there was too much cruel beauty for us to close our eyes. I could have stopped there. I should have. But meanwhile the moon sank below the sharp edge of the world.

15

Dawn brought rain, a soft rain from light clouds. The air on the damp sheets tasted of water when I opened my eyes. Raising myself on my elbow, I looked at Achilles. He was stretched on my bed like a sleeping lion, arms and shoulders relaxed, skin dark as honey. His smooth fair hair on the pillow. Achilles, Achilles. I softly whispered his name, and as if hearing me he shook, a long shiver from neck to hip that I caught in the palm of my hand. I lay down again beside him, my hands on his shoulder blades. 'My love,' I murmured, not even knowing who I was addressing. Rain rustled outside the window like a falling veil. I turned to look at the rain and saw a long empty shadow among the trees. 'My love, my love,' I whispered, but the shadow vanished. Made of stuff of dreams. I lay down again and rested my head against the back of Achilles. I was safe there. Rain caressed the roof and I slept.

I don't know what time it was when I woke because there was no sun, but Achilles was already dressed, sitting by the window, watching me. Pushing away the sheet I sat up. I did not want to smile.

'I'm going today.'

I nodded. 'When?'

'As long as it takes to bridle the horses.'

'I'll come and see you off.'

His eyes were the deep distant colour of musk that sad morning. And in the far distance a clap of thunder ripped the weak fabric of the sky.

'You didn't come the other time,' he said.

'But I know this will be the last time.'

He came to sit on the edge of the bed. I watched his eyes, which at that moment were almost blue. Like steel. I could have spent all the time still left to me motionless like that with my arms on my knees. Watching him. He seemed about to speak, but kept quiet. Stroked my cheek with his fingertips. Then he leaned forward. I waited with my eyes open for his kiss, but it did not come, leaving an empty space between us. Then he got up and went away.

*

The horses were pawing the shining stones of the courtyard. Nine horsemen as always for Argos, Phthia and
other princes and kings leaving Sparta in dust settled
by rain. Achilles in the lead, his arm raised in farewell.
Hair wet and darkened, eyes expressionless. I raised my
arm in response from the top of the steps, my lips pursed.
Though I did not know it I was sure this would be our
last farewell. He pulled on the reins and turned his horse.
And the riders vanished through the gates towards where
the mountains of the Peloponnese were hidden by
persistent drizzle. I bit my tongue, wanting to believe
that the pearls of water on my eyelashes were rain. I'm
made of stone. The door behind me was guarded by two
young soldiers with identical faces, colourless in the weak
light under their bronze helms. When I took a step
towards them they beat their lances on the ground.
Saluting their queen. Not a madwoman, not an adul-
teress, just Helen of Sparta, whatever the wolves of the
council might think. Beyond the soldiers, in the corridor,
was a dark shadow, an emptiness. I walked towards it.

Menelaus returned that night, and the sequence of
unchanging days and evenings began again. I try to
remember those first years of my marriage, my husband's
face on the pillow and the exact quality of his voice. But
I can't. For me, Menelaus only inhabited the edge of days

lived on my own. Perhaps it is only now that I realize he was afraid of me. Ashamed of himself, and with a pathetic, empty pride in the throne he had only been able to occupy as my husband. Brother of the king of kings, but born to be second. And I, as the bards loved to sing, was the most beautiful and also the craziest queen in Greece. There certainly were things to be afraid of.

When the coming of winter brought the wolves down from the mountains and turned the courtyard white with snow, my evenings became empty vigils by the brazier. I could hear again the words of Achilles: *Don't burn.* A man had come from far away and told us at table that Diomedes had married Aegileia, Princess of Argos. Diomedes lost. The childhood I never had finally came to an end there, in those flat words. As if I had ever believed Diomedes would come back. As if it had ever made sense to hope for it. I could feel the memory of him I still held inside me, depressing my spirit as it took its farewell and left me, as I watched him disappear. I locked his voice and face behind iron gates deep down in my soul. To prevent them returning to wound me. From the corner of my eye I could see my unclear reflection in the mirror. Hair pulled together under a gold circlet. Dress of heavy blue wool. I was beautiful that day but Achilles was far away and could not see me, the wrong side of mile after mile of rough impassable sea. He could not know that I had obeyed his word, and that even in those grey nights I was searching inside myself for springs to nourish what had brought him back to me. But he had also gone again leaving no trace, and in spite of my fiery spirit I had not been able to follow him. Or had not wanted to. I looked through the window at the countryside sunk in grey and black. At the veiled night sky, its stars blotted out by snow. I placed my hand on my stomach. And there, under my open palm, I could feel a tiny tremor. It was too soon, I must have imagined it, but I knew then that Achilles had not left me. I wanted to smile, but the air was too full of sadness. A sort of melancholy suspense. Grow little Achilles, I whispered to my belly, grow and come to rule Sparta. It's my kingdom, and I shall leave it to you. I can do that. I'm not like all these men, some easy-going and some severe but all weak. No. I'm like your father. Strong. I'm made of stone. And of fire.

16

From the moment he heard about the child, Menelaus left me alone. Happy, stupidly satisfied by what he saw as a job well done, he would come to my room in the evening and sit watching me weave or spin. Or, with his hands clasped together, just gaze out of the window at the Peloponnese blanketed in snow. When he began to feel sleepy, he would stretch his arms, then interlace his fingers on his stomach. I did my best to ignore him, because I knew what was likely to follow. In my irritation I would work feverishly at spindle or shuttle, twisting the thread into impossible shapes. My whole body would stiffen on my chair. But it was useless. He would sigh, every evening the same sigh, the deep exhalation from tranquil lungs of life successfully achieved. Then he would get up and move stiffly towards me on creaky legs.

'Helen,' pathetically, as if afraid of frightening a small domestic animal, 'Helen,' he would say again, coming closer, his voice even softer. Then his neck would stiffen in a desperate effort to control himself, his eyes fixed on my work as if seeing it through a thick blanket of fog. Then his hand would land on my shoulder and roughly caress the back of my neck. I would close my eyes, put down my work and shrink away from him towards the window. I could not bear the moment when he would bend over and lay his grateful head against my ripening belly. Other men, most men, ignore their wives when their children are gradually maturing towards the light of day. I should have been happy with this kind man who never raised hand or voice against me, but just liked to listen to what he imagined to be his son swimming slowly in his natal waters and who never humiliated me by going with slave girls; but I loathed him. I loathed him, because I could see in his smile the imprint of the weakness that had scarred his life, the total influence of the shadow and weight of his brother; the expression he wore when he sat on the throne of Sparta, the satisfaction of a man who thinks he has won himself a rise in status. I remembered the pride of Diomedes and the majesty of Achilles. I could have destroyed this man with a single blow of the scissors lying beside me on the window ledge. He never realized how much I hated him,

Menelaus, it was something he could not imagine. He had always given me everything I wanted unasked; I only had to say the word and the treasury would have been emptied to buy purple and gold.

But Helen was no Leda, I was not like my mother, and despite the fact that I was queen of Sparta, and every day faced in the mirror a woman I did not know when I combed my hair and dressed it in ribbons interlaced with silver, yet I had myself woven the woollen clothes I wore, and never let my silent slave girls waste their time in idleness. So I wove and spun and listened to the growing son of Achilles that Menelaus would always believe to be his. But it got harder to keep the fires of memory burning as the curve under my clothes swelled, and I found myself beginning to ask whether the weight below my ribs might not after all be his, whether all that conscientious panting had not in the end brought him victory. The mere thought took my eyes to my scissors and sent fresh poison streaming through my veins, and this at least kept apathy at bay. I waited. The dark winter lengthened into a year with no spring or summer, in which the few jewels on the trees were destroyed by cold on branches swollen with useless pollen. While in the yards priests cut the throats of lambs to find out why the earth was so angry, I stroked the closed corolla of my womb and waited for it to begin opening. When

I heard the lambs bleat I shuddered, and pressing my hands over my ears I could clearly hear the voice of Achilles at my side: *the useless oracles of the gods of the sky; animals, animals is all they are and all they will ever be, because they refuse to take responsibility for this useless blood.* He was right, Achilles, the gods were nothing more than dumb idols in whose names these lambs were suffering, so I gave orders that no more should be sacrificed. Madwoman, blasphemer, they probably called me, but I didn't care, strong in the conviction that my heavy body belonged to Achilles. Meanwhile nature held her breath in a year that refused to behave as men expected it to, though there was no premonition of disaster in that immobility, only a slow patient waiting for a gentle goddess to finish her work. Nature was there in every blade of grass, in every cloud, and knew where she was going. I had not grown heavy in vain. My sealed corolla would open to the light of a new summer.

It was a day of solemn ceremony and empty halls. Menelaus was performing the sacrifices he had agreed to reinstate after months of complaints from the council, and the whole court was with him in the temple. I was alone with my slave girls when I felt a gush of warm water flood my thighs. I nearly cried for help, but changed my mind. No, I didn't want them burning oils and holding my hands. No, Helen of Sparta would give birth alone on the stairs like a stray cat, gripping the balusters so as not to cry out. Helen, stupid and obstinate, would be alone, only her own tranquil ghost with her in the only battle she would be allowed as a woman to fight on her own, with that body born to be bought and sold. Be alone, Helen, but don't cry out, break your nails on the stone stairs; breathe, Helen, but don't think about the one who should be here but is far away beyond the sea. Only you yourself matter now, you and your own strength, Helen made of stone and fire. Rip yourself apart like new linen to release this kicking and breathing weight, this weight that is your own on these empty stairs.

The tension in my legs gave way with a great contraction to one final push, and the only cry that escaped my otherwise sealed lips and mingled with the shrill cries of the mortal creature just born, screaming like a calf to open its lungs. Beginning to die from the moment when, eyes closed against the light, it opened its nostrils to breathe for the first time. A small screaming creature at the top of the stairs. Like a wild bitch I bit through the cord that joined us and dragged myself towards her with my hands. For it was her; a female on the stairs, between legs draped with placenta the cleft of her sex that would one day make her, like her mother before her, merchandise for barter. But not now; today I could touch her with my hands and she was mine. My baby girl on those stairs, eyelids still obstinately shut, on her head a thin tuft of hair stained with blood and fluid. I pressed my baby against my painfully swollen breasts, among the stained folds of my dress. I murmured to soothe her. Sleep, baby girl, sleep with me. I rocked us backwards and forwards together. Ignoring a thin rivulet of blood running from my ankles on to the floor. A trivial sign of my victory in this war without witnesses. Sleep, baby girl, sleep. She did not sleep, but stopped screaming and opened her eyes. Blind eyes barely capable of distinguishing vague shadows in the dazzling light. But no matter. It was my shadow those glaucous orbs were seeing. And I already knew what colour they would be when they cleared. Halfway between green and blue. Unbearable.

17

What Achilles had not foreseen was the boredom. A boredom that consumes without burning, without hurting, enclosing us in cages without bars or walls, eating away at the substance of our days and taking over so that we cannot be aware of it before it is too late. This is what happened to me. They took Hermione away to be suckled by a wet nurse, leaving me alone with my swollen breasts in empty rooms that smelled of sadness.

Menelaus kept his distance, disappointed at his failure to produce an heir. He no longer came to my rooms, and began solacing himself at night with beautiful young slave girls with bodies as yet unstretched by childbearing. His old kindness gave way to a general indifference towards his lawful wife, and I no longer felt any pressure to conceal my hatred for him. His absence from my life was just an inconvenient emptiness, an easy excuse for annoyance. I ate and slept alone, and only my women slaves came near me. There was no point in doing my hair or caring how I dressed, and I very soon degenerated again into the tired slattern Achilles had found.

I tried to work off my rage in long runs over the arid fields and exhausting swims in the cold waters of the Eurotas, though it didn't help. I had one slave girl who knew how to ride a horse, and in her company I was able to while away whole afternoons of otherwise unbearable tedium.

Menelaus knew nothing of these expeditions, nor would he have cared, since I was now nothing more than the woman he still visited regularly twice a month with the sole purpose of conceiving a son. And so I would go riding, bribing the grooms with gold and jewellery, and calling at poverty-stricken hovels in the foothills of the Peloponnese, where I mingled with shepherds and peasants and women worn down by constant childbearing and hard work. They would offer me water and ask for nothing back. The gods they prayed to had no relation to the gods venerated in the temples. If I had been born like them, I would have died after an anonymous life of exhausting labour and been buried close to the door of my home. They had never expected anything else. It was the only destiny open to them. They had read it in their mothers' wrinkles and sucked it in with their milk, accepting their destiny just as they accepted their own blood. But for me it had been otherwise. I had had the chance to live a different life, but it had been snatched out of my hands. Of course I was only flesh, bones and skin just like them, but I was also full of regret for what had so nearly happened for me. No, the only way I could have found peace would have been to burn myself out, reconciling myself to the death in life of so many other women like myself, wives of courtiers or captains, invisible women who at thirty years of age were already weaving their own shrouds behind closed doors. But that was not for me. So I forced myself to run till I was breathless, to swim furiously till I was at the point of collapse, and to try to forget in sleep the emptiness of my life. Weaving and burning the earth under my feet.

Hermione got bigger and came to think of her wet nurse as her mother. It was too late for me to do much about this, and in any case I had never wanted to have children. My body, if a little softer than before, regained its slender perfection. But Menelaus's love for me never returned. He continued to pay me visits, more and more often drunk, his breath smelling of wine and his clothes saturated with the cheap perfumes of other women. I had never loved him, but we had respected one another, and now he was insulting me. When he rolled over on his back snoring with satisfaction, I felt myself little more than a tavern tart, the sort who cost little and are quickly worn out. And no one seemed to remember any longer that I was the queen. All Menelaus wanted was a male heir, and when he had that, even these visits would end. My two rooms, my garden and the desolate countryside beyond the river were my world. Though I still had my ghost walking at my side and lingering silently in dark corners. A presence too real for me ever to feel really alone. Of course I had more than many women had. But never enough to satisfy my fiery spirit.

Menelaus was on top of me, an indistinct bristly shape, grunting like an exhausted wild boar until, with a final spasm, he soiled my thighs. Then as always he went on lying on the bed while I pulled the sheet round myself and turned to the wall. Waiting for him to go away. It had been a bad day, rain surprising me while I was swimming, violent whirlpools grabbing me so that I strained my muscles struggling to reach the bank.

I had been resting my aching legs on the soft mattress when Menelaus came reeling up to the bed. I had heard the familiar slamming of the door against the wall. There was little I could do but shut my eyes and make room for him; the quicker I gave in to him the sooner he would be finished; he was always in a hurry.

When he'd finished having his pleasure, he grunted to clear his voice and began his usual grumble: 'Still no boy children.'

'No, not yet.' My voice was expressionless.

'Maybe there's something wrong with you, woman. You produced a daughter easily enough.'

'There's nothing wrong with me.'

'With me, you mean? Is that what you're saying? That I can't—'

'Possibly. How can we know? The gods decide these things.'

My voice was flat, colourless. His drunken rages were usually harmless. That was why I had my back to him, so I didn't see him raise his arm and hit me across the neck. Then he pushed me to the floor. I fell painfully, tangled in the sheet. He was on me before I could get up. I had nothing to defend myself with, nowhere to hide. All I could do was submit to his blows until he had finished. Then he went away without looking back, leaving a battered bundle by the wall. Something the slave girls could tidy away.

18

A split lip, swollen eyes and purple bruises on my cheeks. With delicate hands Etra stitched my right eyebrow and cut the thread. No broken ribs, she said. She had bound my left wrist to a splint; promising it would heal quickly. I very tentatively swept back my hair and looked in the mirror. The woman I saw was someone else. My scornful smile hurt my lips and produced a dark laugh on the unrecognizable mask in the mirror. Poor Helen. Poor Helen indeed. The pathetic timidity of an unloved husband had suddenly turned to violence.

Someone knocked hesitantly on the door. Etra, embroidering at the window, met my look. She too knew the timid knock of the man who in another life had been Menelaus. I nodded to her to open the door, carefully tidying a few loose hairs away behind my ears before turning. 'Well?'

He drew back, terrified. Now he could see for himself the marks of his violence on my body, he was repelled. A weak man. He sat down, or rather collapsed on to the bed. Giving way completely. Holding his head in his hands, feebly tossing back his lifeless hair.

'Forgive me, Helen.'

So he was taking forgiveness for granted. Admitting he'd been drunk would not have helped. He would have done it again. He was asking me to excuse him, he wanted my forgiveness. I had no feeling for him in his misery. He had used up all my pity. I took a deep breath, then spoke in measured tones, without raising my voice; my wounded mouth still hurting. 'Hit me again if you like, Menelaus. But no, I cannot forgive you.'

Slowly he raised his head to meet my eyes and my composed, expressionless face. I'm made of stone. His eyes filled with tears that he made no effort to hold back. I realized what he was about to do a moment before he did it.

'Don't kneel down before me, Menelaus. It won't help.'

He ran away like a child, like the coward and fool he was. He ran away. Etra came back from the next room and took up her embroidery, which she had left on her stool. As she passed, she imperceptibly touched my arm.

Less than a caress, but more than a consolation. She understood. I turned to the mirror again, and recognized in its depths the eyes of a devastated but extremely beautiful woman. On her wounded features she had painted a cruel smile.

I dreamed of my soldier that night. As usual, I couldn't see his face, but I could feel him in the way one feels the sun, as a physical sensation on the skin. He held me close as he had never done in life, softly murmuring my name. That was all he said. But when I woke the marks of the blows I had suffered seemed to have disappeared. Menelaus would never touch me again.

19

Hermione was tired. I knew it from the impatient way she pulled at my dress, hanging with her whole weight from its folds, out of sight of the members of the council before us. I pinched her arm hard to force her to keep still. She had to get used to these long, exhausting ceremonies, and the sooner the better. Suddenly she was still, with scarcely a quiver. I hoped for her sake that she was not about to start crying. In any case, the tenth anniversary of the coronation of Menelaus required a solemn liturgy: embassies had come from many kingdoms in Greece and even from Asia Minor. The most important absentee was Agamemnon, who had stayed in Mycenae to keep an eye on his wife's latest pregnancy. My arrogant sister had still not managed to bring a son into the world. The joke in the suburbs of Mycenae was that the King of Kings couldn't father boys. I smiled at the thought. Just what they deserved. I remembered the smug way my sister had flaunted her belly the last time I'd seen her, years before! Another girl, to add to the three they already had. A disgrace to the throne of Mycenae. The rapidly dwindling queue of diplomats told me we were near the end. The last ambassadors filed into the throne room between the guard and the council; a dazzle of black skin suggesting that the king of Egypt had sent his usual gift of Nubian slaves. I was sorry; in the cold of Sparta they soon died. It was nearly summer now, but the two chained men were already shivering. Distracted by the black slaves, for a moment my tired eyes missed the slow column in the middle of the hall – last of all came warriors carrying helms decorated with horsehair plumes under their arms. Trojans. Long horsehair crests that nearly reached to the ground. Taller than Greeks, more massively built. The councillors pretended indifference, but it was easy to see their envy. It had been a long time since good blood last flowed between Troy and Greece.

'King of Sparta, we bring congratulations from Priam, King of Troy and Sovereign Lord of Asia Minor, who has petitioned the gods to make the next ten years of your reign as prosperous as the first ten.'

I started at the barbarian accent of the Trojan envoy,

a grey-haired elderly man, though still handsome in his bronze armour. Menelaus on his throne inclined his head with the hieratic gravity the councillors had gradually managed to teach him after eight disastrous years. He sat quite still, full of regal dignity if you didn't know him, but by now he had no secrets from me: I recognized the hungry gleam in his eye as he looked about for gifts. A man of small account.

As if aware of this, the Trojan envoy went on: 'King Priam sends you two Trojan chargers, born wild and tamed by Prince Hector himself. They await you in your stables.'

A nod, but I knew Menelaus was disappointed; he had been hoping for gold. As with Agamemnon, age was making him greedy. He was already thirty-five years old, and the shadow of debauchery under his eyes would never leave him. Old and greedy. And that would be my future with him: watching him sit there unworthily on the throne of my ancestors.

'Helen. . .' It was Hermione, one murmur among many that had run through the hall at the arrival of the Trojans. By now, after so many years the wound in my heart had healed, and was nothing more than a dull pinprick, not even a pain under my ribs. 'Helen', never 'Mother'. Despite myself, I was getting like Leda: 'Quiet, Hermione, it's nearly over.'

'I want to see the horses too.'

'I'll take you to see them later.' But I knew she'd soon forget all about it. Hermione had the memory of a fish: it never held anything for long. She was eight years old now, and had the mind of a child. Not stupid, just absent-minded and changeable. Sometimes I wondered how long she would have remembered me if I'd gone away. I looked back at the throne. The usual exchange of blessings and invocations of the gods. At the banquet that followed the Trojans would be seated to the right of the king. I could already see Menelaus drinking with them through the evening, then dropping a discreet order to the steward: the ambassadors would find the most beautiful female slaves in Sparta waiting for them in their beds. Menelaus was afraid of Troy; when their conversation ended, the Trojan envoy barely inclined his head.

Suddenly a sentry cried out and an unknown man thundered through the crowd on horseback: 'Greetings, King of Sparta!'

A silver voice, hair the colour of wet sand, bronze skin. Clear, shining eyes. A straight nose and sensual mouth. Powerful, extremely handsome arms emerging from an embroidered purple tunic. The arms of a statue or a god. But it was a man who dismounted before the throne and handed the reins to Menelaus, who was curled up on his stone throne, barely able to refrain from lifting his hands to protect his face. As if the unknown man might draw his sword from its ruby-encrusted sheath and cut his throat where he sat.

'Gifts from my father, Menelaus. It seemed a shame not to let you see them at once.'

I found it difficult to tear my eyes from the figure of the Trojan prince, and my ears from his barbarian accent. A real man's voice, I thought. And I let myself be beguiled.

Then, like a teacher calling to order an unruly pupil, came the voice of the Trojan ambassador, his mouth twisted into a grimace of annoyance. Ignoring him, the prince bowed politely to my husband and introduced himself: 'Paris, son of Priam.'

Menelaus opened his mouth, then shut it again uncertainly; I silently prayed that he wouldn't start babbling. Menippus took a quick step forward and saved the day: 'On behalf of the Council, prince, welcome.'

Paris barely inclined his head; what a delicate long neck, what a fine contrast with the muscular shoulders just visible under his light linen tunic! Unlike the others, he was not wearing a cuirass, just that valuable sword, a clearer sign of his rank than any armour. I could not imagine blood on those beautiful hands. A man bringing peace, perhaps, after so much cold warfare? Was this Priam's designated heir? The guards came to take the horses that, docile, allowed themselves to be led off; Paris first letting his hand linger tenderly on the neck of the one he had been riding, as if in farewell. Then he turned his fine head and his starry gaze took in the sad hall of Sparta which had never before seemed to me so bare, so empty. So wretched. But those shining eyes ignored that severe Spartan poverty, running past the lines of councillors and guards and ladies and wives. And over the blonde head of Hermione. They finally stopped on me.

20

My arid womb flowed again with the forgotten warmth of desire; my skin seemed on fire and my flesh was throbbing. Imprisoned by his eyes, I could already imagine his hands and his body on top of me and inside me, and I longed to feel the warmth of his tongue in my mouth and the soft contact of his lips.

But our fantasy union was interrupted all too soon; my slave Callira had to drag me away by the wrist, because taking my eyes off that sun was as painful as saying farewell to the sky. As soon as the door to my apartment closed behind me, I ran panting to the mirror. Its uneven surface mocked me with the face of a prostitute. The fashion that year was for heavy make-up and showy jewellery, and since I no longer cared what I looked like, when I had to appear in public I let my slaves do whatever they liked with me.

My hair was built up high in a complicated style constructed round a hairpiece from the north and decorated with pearls; my wrists were overloaded with bracelets, and I was horrified to see a glitter of gold round my throat. They had collared me at last. Furious, I tore everything off and cried out because there was no water in my basin. I had to wash off that mask that was nothing to do with me, tear off that hair that was not mine, and find again the beautiful Helen Achilles and Diomedes had loved. *No*, whispered the voice of Achilles in my memory, *what I loved was your fiery spirit*, but his voice was lost in the new blaze already consuming everything.

'Callira!' I called, ripping my dress in my haste to tear off the brooches, and by the time Callira had appeared calmly at the door to look at me, I had broken two bracelets and ruined my dress. The slave smiled.

'Come, my lady. What you need is a bath.' My first impulse was to hit her, but her light smile put things in perspective and I could only laugh. She laughed with me, and offered her hand to help me up; she already had a tub of hot water ready for me in the next room.

'The best of slaves,' I sighed, relaxing to the water's caress as she cleaned my face. 'And the best of friends too,' I added while the water washed away carmine and white lead.

She gave me a grateful look and offered me a towel.

I stretched out on the bed while she gently dried my back and hair.

When she left the room to fetch the oil, my thoughts returned to Paris. The thighs below his tunic, his knees and his wrists ... his image engulfed me like a wave, overwhelming me with an intensity unlike anything I had ever experienced before.

I should have searched for and found the enchantress beneath those layers of boredom, so that I could have shown him the real Helen that evening, restored to the glory that had once been hers, with the last ten years of my life burned away like an oil lamp; but now stop, enough. I had not noticed Callira's return, but she was running her hands lightly over my body with caresses that went deeper than my skin, reaching muscles and veins, relaxing knots and easing my mind. It seemed quite natural when she ran her fingers along my thighs and touched the damp softness between my legs. I shivered. She pressed her lips against my shoulder, submerging us both in the dense cloud of my desire.

I ransacked chests to find the clothes I had worn nine years before, simple and elegant tunics now completely out of fashion, but rediscovering them was like finding a second skin. I put fine kohl under my eyes and pearls of amber in my hair, but Helen's lips had no need of carmine. In the mirror a remembered shadow become flesh again and smiled at me. Yes, this really was Helen; beautiful, agitated and nervous before the banquet. Callira smiled and allowed one single ornament for my arm, a silver bracelet shaped like a serpent. Callira, Callira; a princess among her own people, and if I had been able to bear losing her I would have sent her back to them. But I was selfish, and she was always smiling; not faithful in the normal manner of slaves, but close to me with a closeness I could not explain except by saying I responded to it. We had come together by strange oblique routes, but we belonged with one another. Which was why I let her push me through the door into the garden, offering me the chance of a little peace before facing the megaron hall full of overexcited men who had eaten and drunk too much, and from whom I would need to distance myself once the dancing girls chosen from the best brothels in the city had made their triumphal entry. Yes, Sparta had brothels: the best in Greece, it was whispered. Closed behind simple wooden doors were luxury and pleasures private citizens would never otherwise have allowed themselves. And this secret licentiousness became politics when served up at the king's table. Now I found myself out of doors, a shawl over my shoulders, the sunset fading to a familiar violet. I realized, not without a certain creeping of my skin, that the sky was like that evening when, so long ago, Diomedes had come to look for me. He too had galloped on horseback into the hall without a thought for anyone, and had chased away ghosts which had now come back to me. But where was my special ghost as that evening silently turned to night? Was he perhaps that shadow descending through the trees and moving away towards the Eurotas? Till that morning I too had dwelt among the misty regions of death, barely lit by occasional lightning flashes. But then I had seen Paris, and life had recovered its value. The living cannot spend long periods with death. In the end, we have to choose.

I had not expected to hear anyone behind me, but was not surprised. A steady step and a calm voice, 'Helen.'

I turned. I had no mask to hide behind now, only the dress I myself had chosen. Paris from Troy was smiling. He was not wearing a sword, only a short cloak that he took off in a single elegant sweep and laid on the ground. I would not be at the banquet that evening.

21

How strange were my flesh and skin, how strange the blood in my veins. How strange my muscles melting like snow at the slightest touch from Paris, how strange that my nerves were at rest when I was with him, how strange that my mind was either totally absent or drowsing in suspended time that he controlled. The time of Paris. The most vivid time of my life. A few days that carried my dreams and hopes to their highest point. Before a gradual decline.

Together. Every night and every day. Paris put off his departure, fascinating and entertaining the king, radiating charm like a fan or wrapping it round everyone like a veil. At the banquets he was a god in my eyes. Even then he was already using the slave girls after supper, but I ignored that, because it was only to fool Menelaus, to stop him suspecting anything. When Paris came to find me in the garden or in my rooms, I was the only one who mattered. I worked through all my clothes and asked for more. Four months he stayed in the palace at Sparta, and every day had a new dress to tear off me with his teeth, every day a new jewel to knock on to the marble floor during our violent love-making. Love was a word Achilles had never used, but Paris spread it about liberally like the petals of ceremonial flowers, making it blossom when he murmured it in my ear, yelling it at the empty countryside when we galloped across the river.

Menelaus saw nothing, or pretended obstinately to see nothing, paralysed in his ineptitude, stifled by his fear of Troy, perhaps even hoping that now at last I might conceive the son his sterile loins had failed to father. The time of Paris was nearly over; I could read that in the rapidly changing weather as it hastened towards the end of the navigation season, and in the impatient step of Amphitryon, the Trojan ambassador, as he diffidently passed down the corridors with his crested helm under his arm, determined always to do the right thing. I knew he had persuaded Paris that they must leave; Paris, my poor child of a lover that I thought perfect, my poor sweetheart of counterfeit gold. But I paid no attention, snatching the hours from the gods' hands with the desperate hunger of a nine years' fast, and emptying the chests to cover myself with purple and pearls so Paris could have a new Helen every day and never tire of me. A Helen silently cutting herself off from her ghosts in the silvery whirlpool of his laugh, in the flame of his foreign touch, further and further from where her true image lay forgotten in the depths of the mirror. Helen, Helen, where are you going? What did you not know, what did you not understand? Like Hermione, I now had the memory of a fish. I could no longer remember what I had had or what I should do. What final reckoning would destiny expect me to pay?

Then a ship with black sails came and brought me hope. Messengers rode in through the courtyard gate crying out their grief to the unresponsive Peloponnese. A king had died.

Menelaus had to go. What else could he have done? Forget our long friendship with Crete, ignore all that mourning? And the splendid presents the Cretan king had sent him only a few months before . . .

My lips devoured the body of Menelaus with a passion they had never felt. While he groaned and writhed I made my hands caress him and my body slither over him, my mouth whispering sensible words in his ear. 'Menelaus . . .'

I caressed him with his odious name and opened my knees to him with husky false sighs. 'Menelaus ...' Thinking of other things, I arched my body and sank my nails in his back, crying out in triumph because I knew I had won when with his protruding belly crushed against my stomach I murmured in a voice exhausted by simulated pleasure, 'Will you go?'

And he answered: 'I will.'

A voluptuous sigh escaped my throat; my fingers gripped him like talons, and all suspicion was banished from his mind as the perfumed sea of my flesh again began moving under him.

22

The king departed. Paris apologized for not being able to leave with him, but unfortunately his ship was not ready, though they certainly would have to set sail in a couple of days; it was the last chance, the sailing season was nearly over, they couldn't allow themselves to miss the last wind for Troy, but of course the hospitality of Sparta had in all respects been . . .

Lengthy farewells followed at the bottom of the steps, with the long procession that would accompany Menelaus to the Cretan ship. The Trojans came too to speed him on his way, Amphitryon frowning despite his prince's promise that they too would be on their way very shortly. In the light breeze of late summer I bent to kiss Menelaus with feigned reserve, my head and neck wrapped in a shawl – 'I'm not well, my love, a bit of a cough, I'm sure it'll pass' – then a step backwards to allow him to climb into his carriage – a carriage rather than a horse for the lazy king of Sparta. The whole court presented arms in salute, Menippus severe, helm under his arm, the perfect mirror-image of Amphitryon who, no coincidence, was at his side. Menelaus had entrusted the court to Menippus, who had his eye on Paris like a guard dog watching a wolf wandering outside the courtyard gate, pretending indifference but already fully aware of what he's after. Feeling the suspicious gaze of Menippus on my back, I bowed my head in a feigned attack of coughing, the better to be able to hide my face in the folds of my shawl. Menelaus saved his last farewell for me, the proud radiant look of a king convinced he was leaving behind a devoted queen, whose only thought was to long for his return home to her bed. I'm sure he mistook my lowered eyes for modesty at the thought of the unbridled pleasures of the previous night, and he signed to the coachman to start with the expression of a satisfied conqueror. From the folds of my shawl I watched him disappear down the road, feeling the poison of success beginning to boil in my veins. The fool had gone and victory was near. When the members of the council who had gathered to honour the king's departure disbanded, chattering, I gave a sigh and ran up the stairs.

'I don't feel well, Menippus,' I told the captain of the guard. 'Tell the steward to look after our guests; I must rest in my rooms.' Menippus curtly inclined his head and took leave of the Trojans with the faintest indication of a bow, but without even deigning to glance at them. But Paris's smile never faltered; we had already reached an agreement. When I reached my rooms I called for my slave women. Only Etra and Callira were to come with me; the rest had to stay behind for the sake of Hermione. They nodded in brief acknowledgement; I had always treated them well; now they owed me one last favour. I had left them enough jewels to sell discreetly so that, once the waters had grown a little calmer, they would be able to buy their liberty. They were to say that before I left I had sent them to look after Hermione, who was indeed in bed with a bad cough. I said goodbye to each, embracing them one by one as they filed past for me to place in their grateful hands the packages containing the jewels. Then they departed and I was left alone with my two trustiest slaves.

'Are you sure, my lady?' asked Etra calmly, looking expectantly at me.

'Sure as never before, Etra. I had to experience death before I could decide to take my life into my own hands.'

She nodded. An old and wise woman, she had lived many lives before this one. She went off in silence to do

my packing. Callira stayed to help me choose the stat-
uettes, combs, veils and other precious and fragile things
I wanted to take with me. Sitting side by side on a mat,
we wrapped images of the gods and Egyptian mirrors in
thick cloths. A chest lay open beside us. We did not speak
as the empty wooden box gradually filled and day passed
outside the windows. When the last red rays left the
wall, Callira's slender hands stopped on the bundles as
if at random. She raised her head.

'Everything all right?' I asked her feverishly. This
moment on the verge of a new life was neither hers nor
mine; just something we had to live through together.

'Our last evening in Sparta,' she said calmly, lowering
her eyes again.

'Will you miss it?'

'Why should I?' She spoke in a proud voice. Sparta had
been her home as a slave. I took her hand: 'When we are
safe, far from Sparta, I'll set you free.'

She shook her head. 'Not now. I shall die free, Helen,
but my freedom is still far off. I must come with you,
that is what my heart tells me. And I'm in no hurry.'
Her smile was beautiful in the twilight as she fastened
the chest with leather straps. Etra came to say she had
finished too, and we hid the luggage under the bed
together with their own simple leather bags. Our cloaks
were ready, so were leather boots. All we had to do now

was leave. A knock on the door, and two slave girls from the kitchen brought in our supper. I ate very little, then wrapped myself in my shawl and went into the garden. The last light of day had gone; all that was left, still ahead of us, was the glimmer from the noisy windows of the banqueting hall. No doubt the steward would have prepared everything well. The farewell party for the Trojans, even in the absence of the king and queen, would be sumptuous. Paris's plan was to fall asleep drunk in the middle of the hall. The guards would then carry him to his own rooms so that Menippus, who now in the absence of Menelaus had more reason than ever to keep an eye on me, would not suspect anything. Paris! I could imagine him laughing, his strong fingers lifting the cup to his lips. My longing for him was burning my veins, and I was certain in my heart that all the love I had given him so far was nothing compared to this. Diomedes, Achilles and my nameless ghost had walked among the twisted branches of the olive trees. I had refused Achilles when he asked me to run away with him, but I was weak then, carrying deep inside me the knowledge and relentless fear of boredom. Ten years of living death had persuaded me that I would rather burn now than be extinguished.

From below, beyond the trees, I could hear the murmur of the Eurotas, a gurgle that grew in my attentive ears to an echoing roar, a memory and a song without music telling of what had been: of Leda's death two years before in Cephalonia giving birth late in life to the child of an unknown man, of the steps of my vanished ghost, of the slow exhaustion of passing time, and of the spirit of Sparta . . . I heard all this and much more in the unsanctified song bereft of nymphs or gods of the Eurotas, in the thunderous silence of water on stone. One day, many years from now, Sparta would fall and the river would be jammed with dead bodies, leaving nothing of that song but a murmur of mourning; but not yet. This evening that had so silently turned to night was mine, and the river was singing only for me, who had made up my mind to leave for ever. It was a sad song, because I would never again feel the water of the Eurotas cool my skin or know it as a backdrop for sad evenings. The river was my boundary and tomorrow it would be my escape route. Its angry current dragged pebbles through the valley to a piteous death in the sea. Water, earth and stone. Yes, that was my spirit. A spirit of stone. Like the Eurotas.

23

Hermione's eyes were shining with fever when I went to her. She stammered something I could not hear, and I held a cup of water to her mouth. She spread her tender lips to drink, then leaned her head against my supporting hand. I looked into her face: the soft, round face of a little girl with fine fair hair; but under her light brows the implacable eyes of Achilles, and the line of her nose hinted at his power. She had nothing of Menelaus in her; I was astonished no one had ever guessed her origin, but these days no one ever looks at little girls. Men only ever believe what they want to believe, and they only want to believe what they can accept. So Hermione had to be the daughter of Menelaus and Helen, born under the evil star of our misbegotten union. Niece of Agamemnon and Clytemnestra, marked with the blood of an ill-

omened line; niece of Castor and Pollux and their incestuous and forgotten love. The destiny of Achilles was still
suspended in the future, but no destiny would ever be
able to change the divine eyes above those rounded cheeks
and that tender chubby body.

That evening as I watched Hermione I realized it would
probably be the last time I would see her. Paris didn't
want her; he only wanted children of his own with his
own gentle nose. And I told myself that with her fish-
like memory Hermione would soon forget the woman
she had never called mother. They would tell her I was
dead and that I had been a bad woman.

But goodbye in any case, and patience, little girl with
your eyes bright with fever, eyes I had thought could be
the key to a new happiness.

I left you when it was still too soon for me to decide
to defy Paris and carry you away wrapped in my cloak.

I touched her cheeks and kissed her sweaty brow,
letting my lips linger a long time on her damp skin. It
would be my last memory of my daughter. She murmured
something more as I was leaving the room, but nothing
I could understand. I did not turn before closing the
door.

Then I slept a long dreamless sleep, and in the faint light
of dawn Callira woke me ready dressed, her eyes fresh,

her hair piled artlessly up and her cloak already round her shoulders. A cold morning; autumn was not far off. I wasted no time on make-up, wrapped my shawl again today round my head and held it to my throat, and with Etra following like a shadow passed down silent corridors to the courtyard. From the top of the steps I briefly greeted the Trojans with a few tired ritual formalities, leaving to the head of the council and Menippus the task of the major part of the farewell ceremonies. Benedictions were exchanged, and unwatered wine was poured on the stones to ensure a calm voyage to Troy. A heavy mist had swallowed the Peloponnese beyond the edge of the courtyard, and when the Trojans disappeared into it without looking back, I put on a hoarse voice and told Menippus I was feeling no better and that again today I would not leave my rooms, so that he and the others must see to everything. In the tired light of early morning he must have mistaken my swollen eyes and pale drawn skin for signs of illness, because he answered respectfully, 'Yes, my lady.'

I should have taken thought then, understanding at that moment the significance of what I was doing, I should have read it in the grey eyes of Menippus, but I kept my eyes to the ground and with long silent steps and my shadow behind me I returned without hurrying down the corridors to my room, where Callira closed the shutters and told the guard the queen was tired and wanted to sleep, and was not well enough to want lunch or dinner. Thus we bought ourselves at least a day; long enough, it was to be hoped, to reach the open sea. And in any case, with the king away there was not much Menippus could do.

As soon as the door was shut a hurried precision took over my movements; cloak and boots and a line of kohl so that even in this crisis Paris would find me beautiful. The boxes had already gone, collected by Trojan guards towards the end of the night; they had crossed the garden in dark cloaks at an hour when no one was awake, and under Callira's orders had hidden our boxes among the rest of their luggage together with the bags of the slaves. All we kept back was a leather knapsack holding the few things we still needed before departure. Etra fastened my thick woollen cloak under my chin for me and looked at me expectantly. I nodded. Callira pulled up her hood and opened the garden door letting the older woman go first, then turned to look at me. I signed to her to go ahead and, her knapsack on her shoulders, she obeyed.

Left alone, I turned to look once more at the room that had been mine all my life. The sad, empty bed with its white, impersonal cover pulled up for the last time, and the line of empty chests against the walls. In the smaller room were my bathtub and loom, and a few shelves for linen. Every ornament had been carefully packed and passed to the Trojans for departure; there was nothing I cared for there any more; it looked like a guestroom I had used for a few days and was leaving without emotion. The mirror had reflected me all my life. In the bed I had dreamed and cried out about Theseus, closed my eyes on my ghosts, embraced Achilles and lain loveless with Menelaus. But all this was behind me, and I felt nothing but ice in my heart.

So without looking back I pulled up my hood and went out into the dew-drenched garden. The air was like cold water and the rose-tinted light beyond the mountains gave promise of a cold dawn and small hope of a good wind for Troy. Shreds of mist festooned the olive branches. I strode firmly down the slope while Etra closed the door, perhaps the first time I had walked without slipping or looking to right or left, because every single tree deserved a farewell and because I knew my ghost was walking nearby, and would remain here, separated from me by my own choice and my crazy joy on that chilly morning.

We left the olive grove behind us and made our way along the bank of the Eurotas for the length of a stadium before we reached the ford. The green light under the trees that I had known at other times was not there, the sun was still too low, but when I raised my eyes to look across to the other bank I could see a girl sitting on the ground. She was wearing a white shift and had my eyes and soft hair down to her shoulders. She looked at me with neither hatred nor love, just a kind of calm greeting, and behind her among the trees was a dark form I no longer recognized. I would have liked to raise my arm to bid them farewell, or to call Callira to chase such madness from my eyes. But already they had vanished, visions banished by the gradually lightening dawn.

'Helen?' Callira's voice was calling me, soft and low.

If I'd wanted to go back, she would have come with me. But I had to drag myself away from that chill and from the sharp shadow of the palace that I could still see beyond the treetops. Callira squeezed my hand and smiled, and together, guiding Etra, we headed for the road through the trees. The river quickly disappeared behind us, its voice mixed with the light rustling of leaves and the singing of waking birds. Now the trees were thinning out, and beyond them we could glimpse the countryside. When a noise made Etra jump like a frightened animal, Callira surprised me by drawing a dagger hidden in her belt. She rapidly scanned the trees with cold eyes, her ears alert under her fine fair hair. 'Horses,' she decided tersely and went ahead of us, sheathing her dagger again once we had passed completely out of the wood.

'Trojans,' she announced, her voice still on edge. I moved forward and put my hand on her shoulder. Four horses and two men, one of them Amphitryon. He had not even removed his helm.

'Prince Paris is travelling with the rest of the retinue. The baggage went off this morning; we'll catch up with the others on the road. They tell me you know how to ride; I have orders to proceed at full gallop.'

I nodded. Amphitryon stood still while the soldier gave us our horses, but as soon as I was ready to mount he was at my side to help me.

'You think I'm a whore,' I whispered, but I know he heard, his clear thoughtful eyes full of astonishment. To be really happy I needed his approval. His clear-cut features reminded me of Tyndareus. But he was not Tyndareus; he was a soldier, and barely inclining his head to acknowledge my words, he leaped into the saddle before I could say any more.

24

It took us two days, from Sparta to the sea; we had left at dawn and arrived after sunset, with only a single brief halt. The Peloponnese ran quickly past us; in front of me I had the shining mane of the black horse with between his ears the soldier who was leading us, and behind me Etra and Callira, with Amphitryon bringing up the rear. I was a princess and he looked after me as such. It was not for me to ask whether he still privately thought of me as a whore.

The cold morning became a heavy midday, then evening once more brought chill to the bones as we rode at full speed, even when the horses began to pant, until, when dark fell, Amphitryon let out a shout, the first sound from him since morning, and the soldier in the lead slowed down. So we closed up to ride in strict formation while the sun went down, girdling the earth with a dense belt of fire as the last seagulls screamed over our heads.

'The sea's not far off,' announced Callira, and in fact we soon saw it beyond the final hill, a long path of fire fading with the light; we only just managed to reach Amyclae before the night watch shut the town's double gates. I watched the closing gates cut off the land of Messenia from my sight.

'Keep together,' commanded Amphitryon, dismounting. My slaves and I dismounted too. He looked at us in surprise.

'The horses are tired,' I said, leading mine by the bridle. The Trojan nodded and looked away. I wouldn't have won his respect even if I'd run all the way from Sparta, but at that time I didn't think it mattered. The horse was breathing heavily, its muzzle, neck and sides white with foam, its eyes dilated with exhaustion. But it followed me as I took the road down to the port. At my side an unexpected light pierced the night, and I turned to see Callira with her lantern raised high. She smiled, and I smiled with her, resting my head on her shoulder.

There, at the bottom of the road, was the port and the ship with Paris on board, and we were about to sail off to a new world. I could only smile despite my tiredness and the inevitable smudging of the kohl under my eyes. The noise in the taverns was a signal to us that Paris and his party were arriving. Amyclae was a small port; four jetties with the Trojan ship anchored a little way out in the shelter of the gulf. At the end of the last jetty a rowing boat was waiting for us, with water lapping against wood and stone. Limpets and mussels were clinging tenaciously to the rocks. The man in the boat had no hood, and my heart missed a beat as I recognized his golden hair in the moonlight.

'Paris!' I covered the distance to the jetty and boat in a surge of joy and threw my arms round his neck. My mouth was on his before I could say another word and we fell with a thud on to the wet bottom of the boat, the water making my cloak heavy but I did not care. Paris! Paris! He responded just as passionately, and when we came up for air we saw that the force of our fall had pushed the boat from the jetty, and an oar was floating uselessly not far off. My prince laughed his soft laugh and manoeuvred us closer with the surviving oar. When I leaned over the side and reached out to recapture the lost one, silver fish touched my fingers in the pale light. It was food they wanted, but I felt their cold lips kissing me before they fled back terrified into the silky darkness of the depths. On the jetty stood the soldier and Callira, Etra and Amphitryon, waiting for us to come back. Behind them the exhausted horses, tied to a bollard, were waiting for a barge to come and take them to the ship. The soldier standing beside Callira on the jetty was quick to grasp her waist and lower her into the boat beside me. I met her eyes; she was my friend and accomplice and we giggled. Amphitryon looked after Etra and once he had come on board too we were ready to go. Paris insisted on rowing and while he rowed he watched me, his deep eyes glistening with confidence of my future at his side. Far off, the light of the rising full moon was soon swallowed up in the dark shadows of the ship's hull. Suddenly I was afraid, and sought comfort like a child in Paris's arms while a rope ladder was lowered to us from above.

'Everything's fine, we're safe now,' he murmured into my hair as I buried my face in the folds of his collar, breathing deeply his sweet rosemary scent, now mingled with the smell of the sea.

'Come, my queen, I'm behind you.' He lifted me and helped me to find a foothold on the ladder. My hands hurt; the rough rope crusted with salt chafed my skin, but I tensed my muscles and struggled rung by rung to the top. A kindly hand reached out to me; I grasped it and found myself on deck. The young man who had helped me looked very much like Paris, though his face was softer and rounder and younger, with adolescent muscles barely visible under his moonlit skin.

'Cebriones.' He introduced himself. 'Paris's brother.'

'I don't remember seeing you at court,' I said in surprise.

He smiled. 'I'm not interested in Sparta; I wanted to discover Greece. I had plenty of time for that.'

Paris was behind me. 'I see you've met one of my brothers.' He slipped his arm round my waist. I relaxed against him, feeling I had come home. 'Bed, my queen; it's anchors aweigh tomorrow at dawn.'

'Tomorrow? I thought . . .'

Paris laughed. 'You can't navigate at night. Anyway, they won't have noticed you've gone yet. At first light, my queen, we sail for home.'

I nodded to Cebriones and let Paris lead me below decks by a little stairway. The slow rolling of the ship took me by surprise; I had never been at sea before. Paris took my hand and guided me through what to him was familiar darkness to our cabin in the stern; it was little more than a hole, but soft linen covers and cushions had been laid on the hard planks. He shut the door behind us and I let myself fall on the bed.

'Tonight, my queen, we need not hide.' He smiled in the darkness and sat down on the edge of the bed. 'We'll sleep together till dawn.'

'Till dawn,' I murmured, and already Sparta was a thousand miles away. His hand grasped my ankle, then moved higher. I relaxed contentedly among the pillows. Moonlight dripped slowly on us through a grille in the ceiling.

25

As he had promised, dawn found Paris in my arms, with his head on my breast and his mouth open; through the grille I could now see a grey sky. It was the hybrid moment when light meets darkness, the grey hour of ghosts as my wet nurse used to call it. I carefully rearranged the bedclothes over Paris on the bunk, and he started slightly in his sleep. I slipped on a tunic and pulled a shawl from my bag on the floor. The deck in the corridor rocked slowly from side to side under my feet. I shuddered at the thought of storms still far away. It was not the thought of sinking that frightened me, but of being seasick in front of Paris's horrified eyes. Trying not to think about it, I got lost twice before I found the little stairway and climbed up to a bridge teeming with activity. The sailors, preparing to set sail, were shouting orders in a dialect

I couldn't understand, and they pushed me roughly out of the way. In the midst of this ordered chaos I saw Cebriones in the bows talking to a tall thin man who was frowning, perhaps the steersman. The Trojan prince smiled and raised his hand to me, as if I were legitimately betrothed to his brother. His boyish smile warmed my heart.

I felt familiar fingers link themselves with mine. 'Callira! Where have you sprung from?'

'Prince Cebriones insisted on giving up his cabin to Etra and me. A mere hole, but anyway . . .'

'I doubt it was an entirely disinterested gesture.'

Callira turned to Cebriones, who was watching her as if transfixed. She gave him a smile such as no slave should ever give a prince, and the Trojan blushed.

'He's only fifteen years old, and I don't think he's ever had a woman.'

'You could be the first,' I teased her, but Callira shook her head.

'If he wants me, he'll arrange it.' A shadow passed over her eyes, turning their icy blue into a black sea. So I grasped her wrist on which a little bronze chain identified her as a slave. I squeezed the links and pulled: the bracelet fell to the deck with a tinkle.

'Starting today, you sleep with anyone you like,' I said severely, but my eyes were laughing.

· Callira looked down, then a smile formed on her slender lips and she threw her arms round my neck. 'I want to be with you always, Helen,' she murmured in my ear.

'Even if you go on fancying last night's handsome soldier?' I answered, laughing.

'You know me too well, my queen. But will you let me stay in your service?'

'As long as you like, dear friend. As long as you like.' I took her hand, and together we watched the dawn dispersing a slight haze.

The anchor came loose from the sea bottom with a screeching of its chain, making terrified fish flee from the hull, streaking diagonally through the green water while the sailors hoisted a square sail. A wind was blowing behind us from the land, on our mixture of red hair and fair hair, as friendly Aeolus filled his cheeks and edged us gently away from the Peloponnese. I turned to look back at the jetties of Amyclae and, at the top of the slope, the town gates which were at that moment being opened for the day. I could see the long road to Sparta bordering the course of the Eurotas, and far off, beyond the bare hills, the mountains of what had been my country. But not now, not any more. A dolphin leaped in front of our bows, followed by another and the sailors shouted with joy. Cebriones came up behind us and, his eyes on Callira, told us sailors called dolphins the nymphs of the sea, and saw it as a good omen when they appeared. Now these mermaids were leaping and spinning wide circles all round the ship, as we entered the metallic, wine-dark sea of Greece.

PART TWO
TROY

1

Asia Minor was hidden under a thick pall of fog, the woollen blanket of a sunless day. Paris wrapped me in his cloak and pressed his lips to my collarbone. 'I wish this could have been a sunlit morning. Troy is so beautiful when its roofs are shining.'

At our last stop, at Tenedos, he had sung the praises of his city, telling me how beautiful I would find it when I finally had the chance to see it, with the blue-tiled roof of Priam's palace sparkling in honour of the gods. But just now none of this was visible; only the outline of the fortified citadel rose above the fog; I looked at its severe contour and the narrow walls marking the bare path up to the temple of Apollo and Athene at the very top. Below the citadel's double walls the whole lower town was drowned in the fog that had swallowed up the homes of rich and poor alike. The open Scaean Gates gaped like a black mouth on the lightless afternoon.

'Make no mistake,' Paris said in my ear, 'this is a gentle land.'

But I had my doubts. Behind Troy a dark mantle of pine forests surrounded Mount Ida, and on either side deep rivers cut like wounds through the sandy plain on their way to the sea. Scamander and Simoeis; the stormy black waters of the one dark and bottomless, while the clear, solid stream of the other moved sluggishly over a bed of red clay. This was my new country: a few wooden houses and a stone pier stretching out to sea. Ten men with lanterns showed us the road. A rowing boat had come to meet us, stopping under the ship's side. Messengers had left Tenedos two days before and reached Troy on horseback to say that Paris was not coming home from Sparta alone. I stayed on deck at the tiller with Cebriones. The sailors looked happy, their leathery old faces wreathed in smiles.

The voyage had taken us a month and a half; moving by furtive stages between caves and improbable landing places which could only be approached at evening, we had finally reached Egypt. From there we moved to Phoenicia, whose inhabitants were interested in nothing but their own business, then Asia Minor, where every landing was greeted triumphantly. Only now did Paris lose the fear and sense of insecurity that had followed him ever since we lost sight of the Peloponnese. We had been only just in time. By now Menelaus knew, but Menippus had been too proud to send news to Mycenae; an old guard dog waiting for his master at the door of an empty palace. Distant Sparta, lost beyond the confines of the world in this sea of milk and vapour. My memory of it blotted out by the numbing weight of the fog. I stood wrapped in my shawl, my eyes closed as I let the day seep through my skin and into my memory. A new life. A new home. I tried to recapture my smile and the sense of security I had felt when I crossed the ford. That crystalline world lost in this land without contours.

Familiar arms encircled my waist and I smelt the forest scent of Callira.

'My queen, we're here; it's no longer a dream or a mirage. This is Troy!'

I sighed. 'I'm no longer a queen, Callira. Hecuba is Queen of Troy and Paris isn't even heir to the throne.'

'Are you sorry you've lost your crown?'

I thought about it for a long moment. A white diadem. No. 'No. Menelaus polluted the throne of Sparta, and that disgusted me.'

Callira nodded, looking towards Troy. 'A beautiful city. But gloomy.'

'Do you think . . . ?'

'Our happiness doesn't depend on where we are. Don't worry, Helen.'

She smiled and I smiled back at her as she moved towards the ship's stern. Off to find her Glaucus. Yes, this was a new life and only the fog was hiding it. I must not behave like a child. I touched the amulet of Egyptian turquoise round my throat, a present from Paris. A new start. We reached the pier. Lines were flung to us, and an unstable gangway was stretched to make a fragile bridge from ship to shore.

My head was spinning after so long at sea, and dry land made me giddy; I needed to get used to it again, learn a second time how to walk. Paris smiled and pressed my hand, then turned back to the ship to direct the unloading while I waited on the wharf for Callira to join me. It was cold in the fog, so I pulled the shawl over my head. I heard a light shuffle, barely more than a sigh on the Trojan wind. I turned. A horseman rode silently out of the fog and looked at me. Even on horseback you could see he was tall. A strong face. Great dark eyes that seemed to absorb the meagre light. Long brown hair drawn together in a tail down his back. Strong arms and broad shoulders. He was riding bareback, and when he saw me looking at him he stared back at me for a long time but I could not interpret the expression in his eyes. Finally he tossed his head like a skittish horse, and silently shook the reins to turn his black charger. Digging in his spurs, he vanished into the fog just as he had come.

'Hector.' said Paris contemptuously behind me.

'What?'

'Hector.' He grimaced as if he had a nasty taste in his mouth.

'He was watching me . . . But why has he gone away?'

'Take no notice, he's mad. Spends more time than he should with our sister Cassandra . . . You'll meet her, but I warn you, don't let her frighten you. She's . . .' He shook his head without finishing what he was saying.

I nodded. No more time for talk. The horses had been disembarked. Callira smiled as she brought my reins. Now Troy.

2

We were swimming in nothingness. We could just hear, indistinctly, the cobbles under our horses' hooves. The houses lining the road were as evanescent as shadows at sunset. There was a black shadow at the gates of Ilium. Hector, but he was not waiting for us. When he saw us he turned his horse and went ahead up the road. The light drumming of galloping hooves in the fog was like ghost music. Paris, riding in front of me, turned in his saddle and shook his head: mad, what did I tell you? I smiled weakly, but he had already turned back. I relaxed. There was no point trying to smile in the dirty milk of this air. We dismounted in a courtyard with invisible walls, gates and soldiers. Paris offered me his hand to help me up a flight of steps. Then more steps and another courtyard. It was like Sparta, too much like Sparta.

Callira went off with the rest of the retinue, giving me a last smile before she disappeared, a glimmer of green eyes fading into that blinding lightlessness, leaving me to climb the steps and cross a corridor alone. I could feel Paris's hand in mine stiffen with anxiety. A son who knows he has done wrong coming home to his father. A child who must be punished. But there was no one about and the sentries guarding the throne room seemed carved from stone. Paris gave me an uncertain smile and we went in.

Facing us across the shining marble floor was Priam.

It was a bigger throne room than the one in Sparta, and higher than I thought it possible for anyone to build. Each window was like an immense wound in the walls, or the throat of a fish in an eternal bluish light. The court was assembled on one side, richly dressed in gold reduced to dull yellow by the absence of sunlight. Like a dune of sand and dust the king had forgotten, but his eyes never left me for a moment as I moved forward. The white splendour of the marble under my feet terrified me. But I did move forward, my smile fixed like a mask, a slave's shawl round my shoulders. My eyes were said to burn with a green flame in weak light.

On the steps to the throne stood Priam's huge family. Women to the left, men to the right, and the queen, her beauty overpowered by heavy ornaments of bronze and violet amethyst, showed her character in her haughty, disdainful mouth, just like the daughters lined up at her side. On the steps to the right of the throne were men in armour with richly decorated leather cuirasses and daggers hanging from their belts. The only man not in armour was Hector, who towered over the hall from the top step, in his eyes the relentless hostility of one who either did not know, or knew and was not interested in hiding his knowledge. His tunic was of simple coarse dark linen, but his face was naturally powerful, a triumph of blood with no need of help from gold. I was twenty paces from the steps when Paris signed me to stop, and I became aware that a young man previously hidden from me by Hector's bulk was actually a woman. Extremely beautiful, with Hector's eyes ringed by violet shadows. Her tunic was dark red and her only ornament was the bright gold band round her loose, untamed hair. A virgin of Apollo: Cassandra.

'Father.' Paris spoke, seeming to have almost recovered his arrogance. 'This is my wife Helen.'

The king wasn't old, not yet; and he ran his eyes over my body. Caressing my flanks and my breasts half-hidden among the folds of my dress, my thighs just visible below my skirt. I did not blush. After Theseus, I was used to male lust.

'Well, so this is the famous Helen . . .' Priam was staring shamelessly at me while the curve of Hecuba's lips became increasingly bitter. There was silence in the hall, and I realized the king was making up his mind. If my body passed the test, his impassive smile would grant me the right to live in Troy. Finally his royal mouth spread in a happy grin: 'Welcome, daughter.'

Paris relaxed beside me with a sigh of relief, while the court made obedient noises, taking the king's approval for granted. Then a cry from Cassandra cut through the hall. I froze with amazement and turned to look at her: her open mouth was emitting a single note, like an animal whose suffering is beyond cure. The long note turned into speech, indistinct but savage.

'Burning . . . like a torch, like fire . . . ruin! Burning!'

'Cassandra, be quiet,' the king finally snapped in irritation.

But she was not listening. She slowly came down the stairs, her troubled eyes staring at me. 'Come from the sea . . .' hardly more than a whisper. Then again that tormented scream. 'Come to bring ruin to Troy!'

I drew back. Paris was in front of me. His features contracted, unrecognizable, his voice almost a snarl. 'Go away, get out, how dare you . . .'

But Cassandra was beyond reason and the threats of men. She looked at him as if she did not know who he was. 'You've brought us the herald of death ... you, too cowardly to fight and born to destroy your race ... you milksop!'

'That's enough!' Paris raised his hand, but Cassandra stood her ground, nostrils quivering as if expecting a blow.

'Don't touch her.' Hector came quickly down the steps of the throne to stand beside his motionless sister, who had turned into a Fury in the middle of the hall.

'Cassandra, come on, let's go away ...'

It was as if he had cut a thread. She collapsed in his arms like a broken doll. Her head on his chest, her body still lightly shuddering, her voice almost inaudible: 'The herald of death ...'

Paris turned away in disgust. Priam spoke: 'My daughter Cassandra has been touched by the gods. Never mind her, Helen.' He smiled as though the woman collapsed into herself was not even there. 'And I hope you will soon give Paris healthy sons. My first grandchildren.'

'No!' screamed Cassandra. Who knows what those eyes glaring at me could see. 'No!' she screamed again.

Her brother took her by the wrists, speaking tenderly as he tried to calm her. In the midst of her screams, the calm voice of Hector was like a rock impervious to the waves. But Cassandra struggled against him, her words falling on me like torches of flame.

'This woman will bring fire. And you will die in the ruin her fire causes. Every one of you . . . !'

'Aeneas,' called Hector, and one of the young men to the right of the throne hurried forward. Together they led Cassandra to the door.

'Hector, wait.' Priam spoke with authority. 'You must keep your sister under control. Or I really shall have to forbid her from appearing in public again.'

I could see a flash of desperate tenderness in Hector's eyes before he gripped Cassandra firmly to take her away. The hatred in the look she gave me as they left the hall was like the quick, accurate slash of a knife cutting my heart in two.

The door closing behind Hector and Aeneas smothered Cassandra's cries. The king tossed his head, ignoring the situation. None of the other princes and princesses, or the queen and the rest of the court, had moved. Their faces remained fixed and expressionless. Priam smiled and said with no trace of irony, 'Welcome to Troy.'

3

Wind curling, wind turning, wind sweeping rocks and singing, singing songs of a time with no thinking or desiring, a time of celebrations and banquets, of music softly sounding from instruments; wind singing to warm nights disappearing sleepless at dawn, and sleepless days in bed in the soft, gentle love of Paris. Wind blowing, wind bringing to the coast of Troy waves of cold, freezing spume, winter passing consumed by the same wind. Wind wrapping itself round the hours and stealing them, wind running away with stolen days under its arm and a lost smile in its eyes. Wind, wind spreading music, obliterating Cassandra's cries and closing Hector's eyes. Perhaps deceiving Helen into believing this is a new life. But only for a short time. Only until spring returns hand in hand with the wind.

4

We were half way through a banquet when they came to tell us the ship had come. It was an important day, the anniversary of the king's coronation and the first day of a quiet, tranquil spring. The wind was still blowing but perfumed now with soft pollen and the amber-scented sap of the forests of Ida. The sun was shining through the great windows and rested playfully on the gold weave of my veil.

I looked questioningly at Paris. It was the first ship since the Hellespont had opened again a few days before. The long winter was over and we had emerged into the sun like dazed lizards. Paris tossed his head carelessly as he sipped his wine. That's what the winter had been like, a succession of parties in halls warmed by braziers; and if I could see no softening in the curve on the queen's

FRANCESCA PETRIZZO

mouth, at least now I could sit at her right hand without her saying anything at all. The Trojan court was a colourful oriental magma of secret rivalries, a tissue of minute intrigues of a kind we had never had in Sparta, of precious cloth and gold flowing from the ever-full coffers of the king. A long way from the Peloponnese with its serious soldiers and hard men. There was never any hunger in the countryside round Troy; whenever Paris and I passed in our carriage the peasants would hurry to the road, offering the last fruit they had preserved before the coming of winter and the first fruits of the new season. I myself was lost, dazed and happy with the thousand presents Paris gave me, letting him adorn me and deck me out in any way he liked; every day new clothes and a new hair-do to rumple and crush during those nights that began at dawn and lasted till long after midday. A life of satisfied desire and stunning happiness. Like a cup of spiced wine. Like the long-forgotten smoke of my laurel-burning braziers.

I did not see Cassandra again after that first dramatic meeting. Paris told me absent-mindedly that Hector had persuaded her not to leave her religious buildings any more except in his company. And Hector himself never crossed my path. The heir to the throne was hardly ever to be seen at receptions, and attended court ceremonies only when protocol demanded it. Even then he would

152

be simply dressed and say little, would do his duty and then leave. To exercise an army enfeebled by too many years of peaceful prosperity, or to ride with Aeneas beyond the mountains and over the plains of Asia Minor, to capture horses that he would then ride bareback. Or to spend whole nights in the forest, hunting. Sometimes Cassandra went with him, or so it was said.

The king would shake his head and say nothing. His view was that the matter should be taken care of by Antenor, his principal councillor, a severe man with harsh features and wolfish eyes, much like Menippus. These days Priam did little more than busy himself with court matters and absent-mindedly approve decrees.

To anyone less blind than myself the fragility of Troy's power would have been obvious, resting as it did on the full stomachs of its people and their conviction that they were invincible. But I had brought with me the accumulated hunger of many, too many, years of deprivation, and my first winter in Troy was merely a reckless abandon to the prevailing wind. Until the day the ship came.

When the door was thrown open I turned anxiously, but Paris just smiled.

'Oh, it'll be the usual Phoenicians, my love, come to renew our trade contracts as they do every year, just that they're a little early this time.'

While the herald ran into the room and circum-navigated the long banqueting table, the diners went on eating and drinking without paying him the least attention.

Priam was lying on a throne of cushions, being enter-tained by a troupe of Bactrian dancing girls. He waved the messenger away with an abrupt gesture; he did not wish to be disturbed, annoyed to be interrupted while concentrating with a spark of lechery in his eye. But the herald stood his ground, fighting for breath with his trumpet in his hand, waiting patiently to be allowed to speak. The chance never came. Instead Hector charged into the hall, slamming the door against the wall so hard that it split.

'Father,' he shouted. That was enough. Hector never normally raised his voice, so the whole court stopped to listen: perhaps at last this moody and supercilious man had something interesting to say.

The heir to the throne passed close to me in a whirl of forest-scented wind and planted himself firmly in front of his father. The Bactrian girls had stopped dancing and were waiting in a corner, their silver ornaments hanging uselessly from them.

'It's a Greek ship. They've sent a delegation. They've come to take her back.'

Hector didn't look my way, but I knew he was referring

to me; I knew it from the slashing ferocity of his few words: *They've come to take her back.*

Priam calmly straightened his cushions. For a moment he played with his heavy gold bracelet. Then he looked up: 'Bring them in.'

5

Ulysses of Ithaca was a cunning man. Not intelligent: cunning. A brilliant diplomat but the worst possible enemy. He knew what he wanted and how to get it. It was no surprise they had sent Ulysses. Behind him was a numb Menelaus. They came forward into the room that a little earlier had received me, though now sunlight had transformed the amorphous court crowd into a mass of gold. I knew the effect the royal family assembled round the throne would have, and I knew my husband's eyes would see me at once. Immediately to the left of the king.

Ulysses looked all round, assessing the hall, unastonished with cold nut-green eyes: the marble, the gold, even me. All just as the wolf of Ithaca had expected. But Menelaus, moving forward slowly in his wake, looked uncomfortable, and I could detect sleeplessness and suffering in the dark patches under his eyes and in his thinning hair. With his graceless body disguised in pretentious bronze armour, he was the caricature of a king.

In a single winter Menelaus had aged ten years. Why had he come?

Ulysses spoke, greeting Priam in a voice as cold as his eyes. A man with no conscience. A quick bow and a smile like a polite growl. 'Queen Helen is clearly in good health. Her stay in Troy has done her good. Now all that remains is for her to come home.'

A calm, informal tone. I gripped the arms of the throne and the raw silk of the king's wide sleeve. Priam smiled.

'I very much doubt Princess Helen would wish to undertake another journey. I believe she finds her present arrangements agreeable.'

'No doubt.' Again that smile. 'But her husband requires her to return to him.'

'Her husband is here beside me, Ulysses. And this is her home; you can see that for yourself.'

Ulysses ran his eyes round the great hall one more time. Then he nodded. 'Very well. I believe we shall need something more *persuasive* to convince Queen Helen that it is now time for her to come back.'

He fixed his eyes on Priam, running them past me as though I didn't exist; his pupils narrowed in the strong light like those of a cat.

'As you wish. We shall be ready to make a suitable response.'

I could see the disastrous irresponsibility of Paris in Priam's smile. An inevitable blood inheritance from father to son. But I didn't react when Menelaus fixed his eyes on me and took two steps towards the throne, wailing in the voice of neither warrior nor king, but simply that of a lonely man, 'Helen . . .'

Helen. Under my intricate Egyptian hairstyle, Helen. Looking at the man and his ravaged face and hearing the broken supplication in his voice, I knew I couldn't go back. I looked away, abandoning him to that cold hall of marble and gold. Menelaus looked down. Anywhere else he would have wept. Ulysses turned icy eyes on Menelaus: 'Let's go.'

Abrupt and impatient, but not quite an order. A statement. As if he was not surprised. Menelaus said no more. He turned and followed the man from Ithaca across the white mirror of the floor, past the guards carved in stone, and over the black granite threshold. Hector, motionless on the steps of the throne, turned his head and looked me in the eyes. His own were clear and expressionless, like a dried-up well.

'War,' he said quietly. The courtiers turned towards him in a single movement like a school of tired fish. The Greeks sailed away before sunset.

6

First came manoeuvres. We were wakened next morning by the sound of officers yelling commands and cavalry gathering in the courtyard. I ran barefoot to the window. Hector was riding bareback, his face hidden by a bronze helm, shouting orders with his sword unsheathed. The Trojan army was responding to his commands and falling in beyond the gate. A serpent of soldiers, their armour glittering in the light haze of dawn. Without consulting anyone else, he was starting preparations.

Paris, who had been sleeping in my bed, came up behind me and kissed my shoulder. 'Only to be expected,' he murmured, smiling and hugging my waist.

'He's right.' My throat was dry, and I felt an unaccustomed heaviness in my limbs. I looked towards the horizon, at the red light on the metal sea, as if from one moment to the next dawn might vanish, shrouded in a thousand sails.

Paris laughed. 'Troy will be too strong for them. Nothing to worry about. Go back to bed.'

His fingers crept down my sides to my thighs. I looked out again at the stern unsmiling young man in the midst of his soldiers in the courtyard. The long hair escaping from under his helm was dusty against the opaque metal of his cuirass. It was like another world. But I believed in Paris and refused to see it, to understand it.

A year of respite followed. It was another year before I heard any more about Greece, about Mycenaean messengers, beaten roads, and consolidated alliances. If I close my eyes I can imagine the palace in Sparta without me, Menelaus crumpled on the throne like a dead leaf and Menippus inspecting troops in the open space beyond the Eurotas. And I can imagine, without seeing it, Agamemnon studying maps of the Aegean, checking a list of those of the kings he had summoned who had agreed to come, arming and loading ships. And I can see very clearly, because I knew her so well, the spark in Clytemnestra's eyes when the king departed, leaving her alone in Mycenae. Probably pregnant yet again, but able to expect a very long period of having what she had always wanted: to be powerful and on her own.

The shadows of the Peloponnese. My eyes remember them after many, too many years. The long march to the port at Aulis – I can see that with the eyes of the shepherds lifting their heads indifferently, only to lower them again rapidly, before the loose column slashing its way through the valleys in the heavy confines of a dark evening. All the way to that long grey beach on the Aegean coast. It was Ulysses who told me what happened next, one evening many years later when he was drunk and Troy had been reduced to ashes. With bloodshot eyes and an obscene burst of laughter, he told me about the lack of wind, the inauspicious oracles, and Agamemnon's daughter Iphigenia having her throat cut on the beach like a sacrificial goat. How her blood turned into polluted mud. How Achilles ineffectively tried to use his sword to protect the girl from the knife. Achilles. His ship with the others, the insignia of Peleus on its sail and the child Patroclus in the bows looking out to sea and dreaming of war. And Diomedes not far off with two ships under the banner of Argos. A wind in their sails that smelt of blood, their prows cutting the waves as though slicing human flesh. Heading for Troy.

Either Priam didn't realize it or he pretended not to know. He was so absent-minded he would have been happy to approve anything Hector and the council suggested to him. Antenor and the crown prince shared fierce looks on decisions already taken. Old men called on their allies. Young men prepared to fight. And one by one, Priam's sons fell under the spell of their eldest brother; we watched them give up their showy parade-ground cuirasses in favour of stronger, unornamented ones. Cebriones became Hector's charioteer, directing horsemen both in front and behind from his Hittite war chariot on the plain. Cassandra surprised me by saying nothing. But those who climbed the winding path up to the temple said they heard her weeping at the altar of Apollo.

I drowned my days at the parties which grew ever more frequent after the declaration of war. Not just in winter, but in summer too, I danced away my tiredness and anxiety, so as not to have to think. Looking back, I see that year as a whirl of bright delirium, of faster and faster dancing to blot out the imminent clash of arms.

7

Spring again. And once more that vague promise in the air of new days and longer sunsets, with the chill slackening its grip until it could do no more than caress my bare shoulders when I went out into the composed, elegant dawn of the palace gardens. In the little artificial lake goslings slept on the stones, while fish slid silently under the water, streaking with dark red the transparent glass of invisible currents.

I sat at the edge of the lake humming to myself; Paris had fallen asleep at first light with a satisfied smile on his face.

The water was a clear mirror above a dark muddy bottom. There were shadows, and my face was a pale ghost on the fragile surface. I reached out to touch it, shattering my image into a mosaic of fugitive fragments.

Then I heard a light laugh, and saw the morning sun resting on Cassandra's red hair. I steeled myself to face her anger, but her full lips were curved in a smile:

'They're here.' When I heard her speak, the word madness never entered my mind.

Cassandra was right: they had come. The whole horizon was black with them, and Hector, woken by his sister, was gathering his men for the first onslaught of war. That morning the court awoke to the sound of drums; and by the time Priam was demanding in a loud voice to be kept informed, Hector had already led the cavalry to the Scaean Gates, which were thrown open for the last time.

They waited for two hours, drawn up on the plain for a sun that did not want to rise, until the black line on the horizon moved forward and turned first into a formation of ants, then a sea monster with a thousand arms. Then the keels of the first ships were scratched by the sand of Troy and armed Greeks started jumping into the water from the bows. Among the first was a tall man in black armour that shone dully in the pale light. Achilles. He was leading the vanguard, heavy infantry to meet the Trojan cavalry before the chariots moved into action. Grasping the rough edge of the bastion I watched him, a black insect on the sandy plain; I was still fighting for breath after the long run from the citadel, my ankles aching from the cobbles of the road I had run down in my over-elegant sandals. All the other women had stayed safely behind the second circle of walls to comment on the novelty of war with the sort of bored surprise that for a year and a half I had found amusing, but would quickly learn to despise.

I watched the battle accompanied, from time to time, by no one but heralds sent out from the palace to collect news. They would take the steps at a run then cling, like me, to the battlements, assessing with anxious eyes the throng of tiny creatures four stadia below us. I would tell them in neutral tones what I had seen, and they would thank me with a bow before running off again. In their eyes, though they tried to conceal it, I could detect amazement at seeing me there, my expensive veils fluttering in the cutting wind and my necklace of pearls and silver sparkling in the weak light. I wound it round my fingers, and did not move until the light itself began to fade, clouds like puffs of smoke chasing each other to meet in the middle of the sky. The grey soon turned black and the first drop of rain landed on my right shoulder. It was impossible to continue fighting on the thick, sticky mud of the plain, and Hector was forced to retire. When I saw the rearguard retreat I went down the steps, and from the top of the rise in the road watched the last soldiers return. Pouring rain glued my clothes to my body and turned my hair to heavy rats' tails down my neck, while the water crushed the crest on Hector's helm and streamed down his cuirass, making him look like a demon from the deep. Supervising the retreat in that underwater world, panting with exhaustion and still carrying his darkly bloodstained sword unsheathed, he turned and saw me. He held my gaze for a moment, then turned back to the soldiers and drew his right hand sharply down in a gesture against which there could be no appeal. The sentries understood and closed the gates. While they were being fixed in place I watched the sea beyond them gradually fall back. No shudder ran through me; no flash of lightning, no premonition or sense of certainty to guide my steps towards home or engrave them with a new consciousness. The siege of Troy had begun, but I had no idea what that might mean. Perhaps at that point even Hector thought it might be possible to make another sortie from those gates next morning. Sheathing his sword while Aeneas gathered the men together, he came up to me, followed by Cebriones holding the reins of his horse.

'What are you doing here?'

Possibly the first words he had addressed to me for many months; I could not make out why the dark eyes under his helm were shining so clearly in that darkness.

'I've been watching the battle,' I answered, since with Hector the truth was always the only possible answer. He nodded slowly and took the reins his brother was holding out to him. He mounted his horse and reached down to me.

'Come, I'll take you back to the palace.'

I looked at his hand, dirty with dust and smeared into long streaks by the rain; I could see the long history of the manoeuvres of the Trojan army written in his hard, cracked skin. I entrusted my slender fingers to his powerful palm, and his strong arm hoisted me on to the saddle. He murmured something I did not understand, perhaps in the local dialect, and the horse set off up the road to the second circle of walls.

All I remembered afterwards of that race across Troy was the unreal whiteness of the houses in the rain, and the intermittent line of cobbles under the black hooves of the horse. And touching the skin of my neck the slight chill of the edge of Hector's helm.

8

'Priam won't let them out.'

Just back from the council, Paris was taking off his belt and offering his neck to my expert hands.

'He says we must wait for our allies. Hector's furious. Keeps saying we're in no condition to stand a siege. Nonsense, if you ask me. Yes, that's the spot, go on!'

My fingers moved gently at the edge of his hair, up into his curls and down again, searching for his shoulder blades under the hem of his tunic.

'How did the battle go?'

'We lost the beach, so Priam takes the view that Hector no longer has any right to speak. He says we can still negotiate, though I doubt it.'

We lost the beach? 'You weren't there.'

'What?' He looked at me with his head on one side. 'What d'you mean by that?'

'That you weren't in the fighting today.'

'Of course I wasn't.' Paris was scornful. 'Fighting? What next? This war has nothing to do with me.'

'Paris!'

'Surely you can't really believe they've come to get you?'

'Well no, but . . .'

'But what? Troy's invincible. Don't worry. And don't go on at me about it.'

'But it's your duty as a prince to—'

'Duty! That's rich, from you. What about *your* duty, *Queen* of Sparta?'

Paris bit his lower lip hard as he sat on the bed and looked at me. There was a cutting edge I had never seen before to his laughing eyes. I pursed my lips and answered firmly: 'My duty was with you. I thought you knew that.'

He smiled, but his face was no longer beautiful, and not because of the light. 'Come here then. And *do your duty*.'

'No.'

There were bound to be other occasions. Times when the features of Paris would seem superimposed on those of Menelaus, till it was difficult to distinguish between them. But now he just stayed there, waiting for me. Sitting on the edge of the bed with the hooded eyes of a sulky adolescent. I stayed standing on the other side of the room with my shoulders against the wall.

His shoulders slumped. 'Have your own way.' He blew out the oil lamp and pulled up the coverlet. I waited until his breathing assumed the slow, regular rhythm of sleep. But I did hear the word, in the darkness and silence of that starless night. Less than a sigh yet more than a sword stroke: 'Bitch.'

Stairs were gliding by under my feet; the edge of each step nothing more than the graduated margin of a dream. An unreal wind laced with pearls of rain, and an unreal coarse shawl round my shoulders as in the old days in Sparta. Up and up I climbed, to the lonely summit of the citadel and the solitary tower behind the temple of Apollo. The sentinel nervously watching the Greeks regroup far off on the beach never noticed me passing, and I found the door open and slipped inside and up the spiral staircase behind him. When I pushed open the trap door at the top of the stairs to step out on to the tower, the wind tore ferociously at my hair and grabbed my shawl and the hem of my dress, forcing them to dance. Clinging to the rough stone balustrade, I could see Troy spread out below me on every side like a slow flow of lava, one continuous terrace down to the plain where no Greek fires could be seen. The sea was black and the sky livid in the brutal, inconstant light as a round full moon tried to hide behind shreds of cloud. The wind was driving away the rain but could not touch the darkness invading my stomach and head alike, a sickness. Then two protective arms opened to shield me, two hands pressed on the wall beside mine.

'Helen.'

'Hector.'

'It's not your fault.'

'I know.'

'But I didn't, not till today.'

In the silence that followed, while his loosened hair mixed with mine in lashing our skins in the wind, I tried to understand. 'Thank you.'

He said nothing more but stood with me watching the storm, until beyond the edge of the sea, grasping the edge of the world with leaden fingers and exhausted light, dawn broke. Then I turned to look at him, and found his dark eyes the door to somewhere too far away and gloomy for me not to be afraid.

Paris had been right: Priam would not let them out of the city. The gates were closed, and messengers sent to all Troy's allies. The king was in no hurry. His granaries were full, his wells deep, and his coffers heavy with gold.

Hector drilled the army at the double on the streets every morning. And on that day, the second of the war, I told Callira to take all the stuff Paris had allowed to accumulate over many months in my room, and remove it to his rooms on the other side of the palace. Then I settled alone with my dear slave in my own apartment with its view over the garden near the royal women's quarters. Under the leaden sky I built a pyre for all my clothes, for my new dresses for each day. While Callira made sure all this linen and purple burned to ashes, I sat before my mirror and combed my loose hair with my fingers, and washed away every last trace of make-up in a basin of water.

9

The siege. Passing time can be counted on stones and in flesh and blood. And in the dirty water on the shore beyond the Greek camp, and among the rocks and sand of the plain. Along what began as a fence made from rushes, but as the days pass has grown into a wall of close-planted saplings as Agamemnon refuses to withdraw. Winds blow over the shore, rippling the sea, ruffling curtains and hair and calling to the soldiers, come, come with me before it's too late. The winds whistle round the keels of ships drawn up out of the water, and stroke the sails lashed to their mainmasts. The winds blow but no one follows in their wake because that is how the kings have decided things shall be, because they refuse to go away. This year the Phoenician merchants only got as far as the island of Tenedos, then saw the siege and turned back without a word. The Hellespont is closed and guarded by dead men, because those standing there *in the unending wind are like dead men, as are those who peer over the walls of the city watching them. All stuck fast, fixed for ever in a time warp that has no intention of ending, in a spring that turns to summer and autumn with no one coming or going. Greece is far away and the last winds come and go, tracing a path over the waves that none of those on the beach make any move to follow. The winds press on to Greece and there is no sign of Troy's allies; they make no move, waiting for the greatest power in Asia Minor to crush by herself the Greeks formed up outside her walls.*

Priam issues no orders, Hector runs round and round in circles inside the walls, and Troy waits. Paris is no longer sleeping with Helen, murmur the courtiers, their tireless bored gossip unaffected by the war. Can he have grown tired of her? whisper the female slaves as they bend over their looms. Have you noticed she no longer dresses her hair or wears any make-up, and spends more and more time climbing the steep path up to the temple of Apollo? To Cassandra? The wind swallows their whispers as clouds pile up and the breeze turns to a piercing blast, ripping clothes and penetrating the skin. This gossip inside and outside the walls no longer matters. It is no use to anybody.

The passing wind collects dust and builds it into what seems like yet another siege machine set up against the walls of the city. It is the beginning of the end, but the people don't see that; both inside and outside the walls they are still waiting. The grey sky swallows their voices and the rain of returning winter dispels their images while the forests roar and whisper on Ida. Soon, quite soon, they will start shouting. But not yet. This is only the beginning of winter, and in her dark rooms Helen orders braziers to be lighted. By their red glow Cassandra smiles with perfectly sane eyes as she takes the thread Callira holds out to her, and begins with the two foreign women to weave the first warp of a long cloth.

10

Cassandra had come to me at the end of summer, once it was clear that Agamemnon had no intention of going home. This siege bore no relation to any other; sieges usually came and went with the winds, but not the King of Mycenae, whose army could be seen gathering wood and building huts to replace their tents. Settling down obstinately to a stay under the walls. One day, when yet another storm was fighting to survive the pale, cold sun, to usurp its place, when it was clear summer had slipped by, Callira came to find me in the garden to announce an unexpected visit.

Cassandra approached me with the same strange smile on her lips as that day when the sea had first filled with ships and the sky with clouds. Without saying a word she held out her hand; it was slender and delicate, and I saw that the nails on her tapering fingers had been bitten to the quick. She lightly touched the long lock of hair hanging artlessly against my shoulder.

'So you too have grown tired of complicated hairstyles, Helen from Sparta?'

'Yes, long ago,' I said. 'And you . . .?'

'Why have I come?' She looked away, at the little lake where wet ducks were shaking out their feathers. 'Let's just say, Helen, that what I see and what I would like to see are two different things.' She sat down on the damp grass, pulling her simple woollen shawl round herself. The dark shadows under her magnificent dark eyes told of sleepless nights.

I caught my breath. 'So you've never . . .?'

She raised her clear eyes and looked at me. 'I've never hated you. But the gods speak through me, and I can't control that.'

'The gods are mute,' I said drily. But Cassandra was still smiling.

'Maybe I'm just mad, like you think. But none of us can ever know our own beginning or ending. Sit beside me.' She held out her hand, curving her lips in that enigmatic smile. I feasted my eyes on her tormented fingers but she followed my look and pulled her hand back, studying it as if seeing it for the first time.

'Terrible, I know. I often bite my nails. Sometimes it calms me.' She looked up again, smiling.

I swallowed. There was something I had long wanted to ask her. 'That day when you saw me for the first time . . .'

'I remember nothing of that. I never saw you come through the gates; I was already possessed. It was dark when I came to again in Hector's arms. At home.'

'In the temple of Apollo?'

'Yes.'

'You must love your brother very much.'

It was as if I had kindled a light in her eyes. A secret glitter, like pearls hidden under sand. 'Hector is part of me. I shall weep grievously when he dies.' A shadow of sadness veiled her smile, but the light in her eyes was still there.

My knees felt weak and I sat down on the ground. 'When will that be?'

'Oh, fairly soon. In a few years. But don't worry, he won't suffer much. And soon after that I shall join him where waves break eternally against the shore and all shadows are long.'

Absently, I watched her eyes lose focus on the grass while her tortured fingers lingered, fragile and sensitive, among the stems. She lifted a drop of water like a diamond on her fingertip and offered it to me. I bent down and licked it. It tasted cold.

'Paris doesn't come to you any more, I think.'

A pang in my heart, but it faded. From deep down had surfaced the memory of that day at Amyclae: the woman in the bows and the metallic Greek sea reflecting unkept promises like a mirror. I shook my head.

'You're already not suffering any more, and you wonder why,' said Cassandra slowly, watching me.

'How do you know?'

'One doesn't have to be a seer to know you live with ghosts, Helen. But it's of no importance. Not to me, at least.'

She smiled again, and her ruined beauty was agonizing, a rose withered by early frost before it could flower. She stood up, not bothering to shake the grass off her dress, and looked down at me, a princess despite her simple dress and unkempt hair. Hector's flesh and blood.

'You know the way.'

I had no need to ask what she meant. She slipped away, the hem of her tunic just touching the ground. She seemed hardly to be touching the ground at all.

Cassandra was right. I did know the way, and I often used it. Callira made the most of these visits by going to see Glaucus, their previously occasional meetings now a daily comfort to both. My Hyperborean friend smiled when I teased her about a possible wedding; smiled and set off with quick steps for the lower city. While I went upwards, to the temple of Apollo with its green serpentine pillars, where snakes slid over the floor without biting and silent girls in golden veils made daily sacrifices. I spent whole days lost in its mellow penumbra watching Cassandra direct choirs and receive offerings. And pronounce oracles. She would never do this on demand, but sometimes without warning her slender wrists and long neck would stiffen, and without a word she would grasp the nearest support, her eyes fixed on places no one else could see. The voice I heard at such times, the tortured scream of a dying animal as on that first day, was not her own voice. Her normal voice was low and warm, profoundly resonant. Like Hector's, and it carried the same authority.

By now I was eating meals in my own room, and no longer taking part in court ceremonies. Everything had been said on the subject of my disappearance, and Callira, angrily avoiding my eye, had told me that Paris was making no secret of the fact that he much preferred the court ladies. What did I care. I had simply mistaken an immature infatuation for the great love of my life. Sometimes I saw him cross the courtyard, his handsome body in useless shining armour, and all that was left in my heart was ashes.

11

The door of the temple opened. I thought Callira had come for me. Motionless for long periods, I would lose all sense of time, my nostrils full of the soft scent of sandalwood and my eyes lulled by the oblique light from the skylight just above the altar. More and more often, Callira had to come and call me; silently placing her soft hand on my shoulder.

Hearing light steps behind me, I smiled. 'I'm late, I know,' I said softly. 'But don't worry, I shall come at once.'

No answer. I turned. Hector was facing me from the shadows.

'I'm sorry,' I whispered in confusion, 'I thought you were someone else.'

He said nothing, his eyes shining. He was wearing a leather cuirass and his hair was grey with dust.

'Manoeuvres?'

He nodded and glanced towards the altar. It was the hour of evening prayer and Cassandra, her hands on the red-striped marble, was murmuring in an undertone with her eyes closed.

'Don't let me disturb you,' Hector said, turning to open the door again. Through it I could see blue sky and a red sunset, day and night embracing in the calm of evening. I picked up my shawl and followed him out. The forecourt in front of the temple was deserted. He was already at the foot of the steps when he heard me shut the door and turned to look back. The light was clear, almost summery despite the nip of cold, and I wondered at his bare arms as he watched me from his always unfathomable eyes. Seen from above they were dark wells in which it would have been only too easy to lose myself. A long moment passed before I spoke. 'Priam still doesn't want anyone to go out.'

'No.'

I hesitated, then went down the steps to join him on the forecourt. My eyes took in the slopes of Ilium, the smooth stretch of roofs reaching up to the abrupt crest of the walls. The plain beyond the Scaean Gates was a no-man's-land of dry, wrinkled earth. Soil gave way to sand just before the Greek wall, with their ships lying like lost insects at the edge of a sea already in shadow.

There was no menace in the abandoned sloping shapes of the ships, the men around them hardly visible.

'I'll come with you to the palace,' said Hector suddenly, his voice breaking the silence like a trumpet blast.

I shook my head. 'Callira will fetch me. There's no need.'

He nodded, but didn't move. He too was looking at the sea. There was a hard edge to his voice when he added, 'You don't come to court any more.'

Now it was my turn to be laconic and sad. 'No.'

He looked at me. 'I thought you came to Troy because you were bored.'

I met his eyes. 'I thought I'd come for love. But I made a mistake. And boredom's not something you can cure by changing your home.'

I turned to go but Hector stopped me. I felt him touch me for the first time. Not from duty or courtesy. But to hold me back. I smiled. 'What's going on, Hector of Troy? Has the imperfect lust of men affected even you?' He seemed to have missed the irony in my voice. He was breathing heavily but didn't let go. When he spoke his voice broke. 'Don't laugh.'

'Why not? Like Paris, you'd take me, then go off when you got tired of me. But you've come rather late. Perhaps you should have come to Sparta that time with the delegation.'

I pulled my wrist away from him and set off down the path with a springy step as if I was a child again, feeling strangely weightless as the horizon began to sink behind the uneven line of houses. Hector caught me up.

'I won't touch you if you don't want me to.' His voice was hoarse, his hands hanging by his sides.

'I don't find that easy to believe,' I said savagely.

'Then you've only known worthless men.'

He was serious. There was nothing superficial about Hector, there could not be if he was to live and die the way he did live and die. A spirit of earth, not of fire. I started walking again, and he followed. I could feel his eyes on the back of my neck, every fibre in me conscious of that tense body walking slowly behind me. It was strange to think I had been so quick to follow him out of that door, attracted by the promise of the sky and his silhouette against the clear light. He was beautiful, Hector, as I realized with painful clarity when he left me at the palace gate, his strong, perhaps rather too tall, body moving away from me with firm if not entirely well coordinated steps. No, not all the men I had known had been worthless, but Paris had made me bitter in heart and body.

Don't worry, Helen. There's plenty of time. Hector's not in any hurry.

I started abruptly, still leaning on the door jamb,

intently searching what was now a clear night. It sounded like Cassandra's voice, but I couldn't see her. The wind rose, and I wondered if those constant gusts might not be carrying away my reason. Then I remembered Hector's eyes, and forgot everything else.

In my apartment, Callira had already lit the braziers.

12

Winter runs through cold rooms padded with woollen shawls, while outside in the icy biting wind of Troy, the Greek defences are covered with shining frost. The frozen dew is white on chariots left in the open, and winds have closed the Hellespont. And the allies of Troy, complaining of the cold, have still not come. Priam nods, hanging his head as if he still believes in them. No more Bactrian dancing girls, and no braziers to dispel the foggy clouds of condensing breath. Paris sleeps in a different bed each night, and Helen the bitch no longer has anything to say at all.

13

The path up to the temple was swept by furious gales, sharp-edged shields of cold wind that slashed one's ankles like knives. I pulled my shawl over my head to stop the wind loosening the knot holding my hair in place and fumbling inquisitively under my tunic. The slender Aricia was waiting for me at the gate, her big loose mantle attacked by icy gusts; I ran up the steps and once we were inside it took our combined strength to close the door. The crash of wood echoed through the empty temple like a dismal drum; Aricia trembled and loosened her cloak, and beckoned me to go with her towards the warmer dormitory area.

I followed the young novice, Cassandra's favourite, down a covered corridor and up a flight of stairs. Cassandra's room was at the top. Aricia went in without knocking, then stepped aside to let me pass. Cassandra was sitting cross-legged on the bed, examining the contents of a bowl of metal beads.

'Come in, Helen,' she said without looking up; I laid my shawl on the table and sat down at the head of the bed.

'You can stay if you like, Aricia,' she added encouragingly, but, blushing under her fringe of yellow hair, the girl responded with a terrified stammer.

'I . . . no, thank you . . . you're too kind . . . I . . .' Tripping over her own feet, she fled so that the rest of her mumbled and broken words were lost on the far side of the heavy wooden door.

Looking up, Cassandra smiled. 'An adorable girl,' she said, 'though maybe brought on a little too quickly. She's in love with me; I hope she gets over it soon. When she was still capable of normal conversation it was a pleasure to be with her.'

I smiled too. 'Of course she'll get over it. After all, you're her teacher . . .'

'And sister and confidante. Her family wanted to keep her dowry, I suppose.' Her tone was light, but there was a profound bitterness in her sharp features. Putting aside the bowl of beads, she went over to the mirror. With her back to me she grasped the table with both hands and breathed deeply once, twice, thrice. Her knuckles turned white and her wrists stiffened. I said nothing; in the world of her anger, Cassandra was on her own. I looked absent-mindedly out of the window; beyond the barred shutters the world was screaming a protest at the brutality of the storm. Still absent-minded, I reached for the bowl on the bed and shook it so that the beads sang.

'Aeneas brought me those,' explained Cassandra, suddenly turning with a smile on her pursed lips. She nervously pushed back her hair. 'They made a sortie on horseback beyond Ida. Carrying yet another fruitless message, I expect. He bought these beads on the shores of Colchis. For me.'

She sat down on the bed again, taking the bowl in her hands and turning it three times. Metal hissed against metal like a serpent. Then, her dark eyes nearly black, she turned the bowl one more time as if waiting for something. Perhaps for words in some language I could not understand. I looked away uneasily. 'That was a nice thought.'

There was something in the sudden blossoming of Cassandra's smile, in her irrational swing from one mood to another, that suggested the madness they attributed to her. Now she answered in a dreamy voice: 'The future's simply in the bowl. Better than frothing and shaking, I suppose.'

She was as tough as Hector, and there were no nuances for her.

'The future?'

She nodded. 'The nomads foretell the future with iron beads. I imagine my usual prophetic fits would knock them off their horses.' She smiled again; it might have been a joke, but the beads were still turning in the bowl, and as I watched they formed an indistinct spiral, a chain of grey light.

'Ask,' murmured Cassandra.

So I asked my question of gods whose voices I did not know; the bowl tilted and the grey chain was broken. Beads fell from the bed like solid drops of water, bouncing on the beaten earth floor and rolling away between the legs of the chair. Cassandra watched them for a moment, then began murmuring in a low voice, her lips scarcely moving and her eyes far away. Finally she murmured, 'Ten,' and tightened her fingers slightly on the edge of the bowl.

I felt blood drain from my cheeks and hide in distant corners of my body as if my heart had stopped beating. For a long moment Cassandra went on concentrating in silence; then turned to me again. She reached for my hand; her own was surprisingly warm.

'It is a long time for a war, you're right.' I could feel veins of marble down my back and looked at her, knowing she would be smiling.

'What . . .?'

'Don't ask questions when you don't want to hear the answers, Helen from Sparta,' she said briskly, springing nimbly from the bed to pick up the fallen beads.

'Ten,' she said again. 'And one already gone.' One bead slipped from her fingers and rolled against the door jamb. She left it and turned towards me with the bowl still in her hands.

It was silly to be afraid of a bowl of iron beads, but my skin was unused to the cold and my throat was dry. 'Put them away.'

Cassandra nodded indulgently, and bowl and beads disappeared into an engraved wooden box on the table. The uncertain light of the lamp captured the soft glow of an amber necklace.

'Was that a present from Aeneas too?' My tongue was running away with me, and I felt I must pay a price for my fear. But Cassandra was not disconcerted.

'Aeneas son of Anchises has often brought me presents. And I have accepted them whenever possible.' I could not read her expression; her eyes as she sat beside me were fixed on empty space and her hands were round her knees. She rocked herself gently.

'Yes, it is as you think, Helen,' she added slowly, her voice far away, 'but I haven't betrayed the dumb cruel god of these walls. The love of mortals is a small thing; though it can warm you, even at a distance.'

Suddenly I remembered my first day in Troy; the hands of Aeneas on Cassandra's wrists, removing her with gentle force, and the endless military manoeuvres of Hector through the streets, Aeneas behind him with a dark shadow under his eyes.

An ant slowly began crossing the floor as though it had all the time in the world. And perhaps it did, since it could not know that it must die.

'He was happier once, even though he knew the day must come when the doors would close behind me. He used to smile, did Aeneas, a lovely smile. But Hector never smiled, even when we were children. They call me mad, but Hector knows. He has no need of shouting, no need of laurel.'

Suddenly she looked up, and in the dying light from the lamp which had almost gone out, her eyes had neither pupils nor colour.

'Forget Paris, Helen. But don't run away.'

I'm certain she could no longer see me when I got up and went to the door. She did not move but was softly humming a slow tune, her eyes fixed on the ant still on its way across the room.

14

I had never welcomed the wind of Troy so sincerely as when it assailed me fiercely at the gate. I didn't even hide behind my shawl but let it attack me and bring tears to my eyes. I could barely see a couple of steps in front of me, and the sea was a black abyss with the power to sweep away the entire Greek race. I was alone in the cold, alone in a way I had not known for many years; and my grief at the loss of Paris was swallowed up in the wind that pierced my skin, tearing at my muscles till they almost bled. Paris had been my love, I had wanted him and believed in him. I had given him everything; there was no corner of me I had not exposed to him, revealed to him. And one offence had been enough to make him want to detach himself from me, and return to what, Callira whispered softly that evening, had always been his real life.

Disillusion and scorn had provided me with a safe haven and sealed my wound with stitches of fire, but now the wound had come open. I dropped to my knees on paving stones as cold as the invisible sea beyond the wind. Paris. I hated the memory of his body on mine, corrupted for ever by his estrangement. I tried to remember his face on that moonlit night in the port of Amyclae, but the wind slashed it away, bringing back my moans and his, distorted, destroyed by the lamentations of an impure love. I had believed it was real love, I wanted to shout; and months of denial were turning in me a dagger of silent fury. The wind mocked me with long-ago memories of the eyes of Diomedes and the hands of Achilles, destroyed from one day to the next without me even noticing, and superimposed on the unbelievable eyes of Achilles were the eyes of Hermione whom I had left behind for ever, and my abandonment of her stopped my throat and took away my breath.

Diomedes. Achilles. Hermione. And my nameless ghost swept away without regret or scruple by the wind. Hermione. Achilles. Diomedes. My mourning dirge emphasized the stupidity of my mistaken flight, the only thing I should have said no to. But I had been hardly more than a child then, a voice inside me tried to implore, all pride lost; but the only reply that came on the wind was the mocking voice of Theseus returned from the dead to torment me: It was boredom, not love; is that what you're saying, Helen, you coward? You know only too well that you'd like to suffer for Paris and weep for love, but you can't do that any longer because your heart was cremated on that pyre, remember? You should have let me carry you off; you're like me, and now all that is left is the imprint of your dead love.

The wind was laughing at me and Theseus with it. It would have been pointless to put my hands over my ears or lower my eyes. I'm made of stone, insisted an ever more plaintive voice; but it was no longer true, and even if it had been true it would have meant nothing.

I opened my eyes to a world of hot steam. I could vaguely remember a woman stretched on the ground with her shawl thrown like a black crow over her head by the wind, and of a man emerging from the wind to carry her away, his arms like dark snakes of unexpected salvation. Beyond that was only the warmth. I opened my eyes to see spears, a whole wall covered with them, reaching from one side of the room to the other. One corner of the room was occupied by a shield, and beside it a helm with a long, lugubrious black horsetail plume.

Hector was sitting on a low stool in the opposite corner; he got up and came towards me.

'How are you?' He knelt down on the floor, his face

close to mine; I could see my reflection in his eyes, a reflection stamped with lineaments of anguish. I wrapped myself more tightly in the coverlet that someone, perhaps he himself, had laid over me. The bed was narrow, but even when I stretched my legs I could not reach the end of it. It was his bed; when he stood up I looked round the room again, but apart from the weapons and the stool it held nothing but a long wooden chest. The Crown Prince of Troy lived in an armoury and slept on a camp bed.

He came towards me again, carrying a cup. 'Drink.'

I obeyed. My tongue shuddered at the sour taste of goat's milk even though warm and sweetened by honey. I emptied the earthenware goblet in a single draught and gave it back to him. He put it down on the floor while his dark eyes, Cassandra's eyes, continued to watch me.

'You were calling out names,' he said in a neutral tone.

I noticed, as if for the first time, how deep his voice was, a rich warm bass.

'A woman, Hermione. Then other names. Greeks.'

'Hermione is my daughter.' My voice was trying to be neutral, but failed, as useless as a discarded scrap of thread at the bottom of an empty chest.

'Did you love the Greeks?' His rough timbre was insistent though he was trying hard, like me, to control his voice.

'I used to think I did. Now I'm not sure any more.'

'Because of Paris.' It was not a question. His breathing was slower, the urgency gone, and I would have liked to describe the shadow behind his words as sadness, but Hector was in any case a melancholy man, and I lacked Cassandra's gift of clairvoyance. I turned my face to the wall, as if by so doing I could negate his presence. He waited a long moment, then took my chin in his fingers and forced me to turn back towards him. I remembered the gentle force of Aeneas holding Cassandra's wrists.

'Look at me.'

Look at me. I did so. He had neither the burning black eyes of Diomedes, the unbearable eyes of Achilles, nor the green eyes of my cremated love, those eyes once so limpid in the star-filled Spartan night. No, Hector's eyes were like gorges, wells dug deep in the black surface of the earth, or shady valleys in woods otherwise flooded with sunlight. They seemed to see right into me, reading, understanding and forgiving. I slapped away his hand, because his eyes seemed to be invading me with a condescending contempt.

'Don't look at me like that.'

He said nothing, but went on looking.

'You seem to be judging me, as though you understand me; I don't need your forgiveness.'

'Nor I yours, Helen; but I'm asking you to forgive me all the same.'

I turned. 'What for?'

He straightened up, a very tall man kneeling on the floor, and turned away. 'I was so happy when I saw Paris go back to being his old self, taking a new woman every night. I was so happy – yes, Helen, I really was – when you stopped smothering yourself in gold and purple and started climbing the path to Cassandra every day. I never thought of the grief that must have crushed you, only of the solitude you had won that seemed like freedom to me.' He bent his head, like the shadowy dark horse that he was, and continued in his dark voice.

'Freedom for you to come to me. And for me to find you in that bed under that coverlet, by your own free choice. You were right, Helen; I'm a man just like all the others, and there's nothing different about my desire.'

He was looking at me over his right shoulder. 'Listen. All I want to say is that what keeps me here talking to you as if I was a child is not your body or your name but the sparkle in your eyes the first time I saw you. I never felt contempt for you, only envy. I never had that sparkle and never could have it. But I wanted it.' He stopped, leaving the last two words suspended in the air like a broken feather.

'Children don't speak like that.' The words came so slowly, so smoothly, so naturally to me, that I hardly realized I had said them.

'Nor do men.' There was a funereal cadence in his

voice, as if he knew as much as anyone and more than most about the death waiting for him round the corner of the road. I smiled, not from scorn or for fun, but from a strange hidden joy.

'Heroes then.'

He turned, and I remembered the first time I had seen his face with its strong features and gloomy expression; it was as if we were back in the thick milky fog of my first day in Troy. In that sea of nothingness where time could curl round like a serpent and return to its beginning.

'Paris doesn't matter to me,' I said in a low voice, and it was true, in that golden light that brought past and future together.

'And the Greeks?'

I didn't answer, I just moved closer to the wall, leaving half the narrow bed for him. He surprised me with a smile; I realized Cassandra was right, because there was even something sad in his smile.

'We can never fit together here, Helen. And I'm in no hurry.'

'Nor am I. All I want is to sleep. With you.'

He paused a moment in his smile, then came and sat beside me. The only way for us both to lie on that camp bed was for him to take me in his arms, making the hollow of his collarbone my pillow and his chest my couch. I closed my eyes in the golden light, and slept.

15

So began the time of my love for Hector, the season of my last love. The siege beyond the walls was merely a background noise, because I had my light and my sun within the walls, my redemption for a life of unhappiness punctuated by rare moments of joy that had always cost too high a price.

Five years passed like this, years of serenity when nothing happened, while Troy headed for ruin with no one answering her call. The Greek huts on the shore grew into stone houses, and the ships hauled up on the sand became overgrown with moss and began to rot. Priam's treasure dwindled and the parties became few and far between. Paris, putting on weight from enforced leisure, hardly ever crossed my path. The whole city knew that the heir to the throne was spending his afternoons after manoeuvres in the rooms of the Greek woman; and the whole city saw us together climbing the path to the temple of Apollo and its obliging shade.

Bitch, bitch, Paris's lovers would whisper as they slipped silently down the corridors, but their words meant nothing to me. What they did not know was that Hector held the wool for me while I was weaving, and the distaff while I was spinning, and that during the long Trojan evenings he would walk with me in the red shadows cast by the sun in the garden – deserted now that the princesses were sleeping longer hours to preserve their beauty for better times, with somewhere else Queen Hecuba sitting studying her hands in silence.

Our world was collapsing round us, and Hector knew it; he knew it from the streets of Troy overgrown with grass because their inhabitants now hardly ever left their houses, exhausted by an epidemic that had decimated them in the third year; and he knew it from the empty Hellespont beyond the besieging Greeks on the beach. He knew it because our allies had not come to the rescue of Troy, and were now falling one after another to the attacks of determined men sent against them by Agamemnon. Asia Minor was the only compensation the obstinate king could offer his tired soldiers. Refugees crowded under the walls discussing Achilles and Diomedes and the anger of Ares.

These names touched a part of me that was vigilant and on guard, and that knew the reason for the sad warning in Cassandra's eyes, and the uncontrollable trembling that often seized her. Cassandra knew but did not speak, and pretended like the rest of us that our make-believe peace, our tiny war-free fragment of life, would last for ever. Hector's hand holding my own was no illusion, any more than the anxious shadow of Aeneas at the edge of my field of vision, nor the silent devotion that drove me every day to climb up to the temple of Apollo where Cassandra would be officiating. People see what they want to see, and no one ever noticed the second-in-command of the Trojan army sitting for hours on the wall in the temple courtyard watching Cassandra teaching the secret doctrine of the future to her initiates, while the seasons slowly unfolded over our heads and the world turned calmly and silently on its way, taking with it the obstinate silent love of Aeneas, the rage he took out on his wooden targets, the furious desire in his blood for Cassandra, and the ill-kept secret in his eyes. But men believe what they see, and in him they saw the blood of their own shattered dreams.

Shut away by that siege whose outcome he could guess, on those garden lawns we still had to ourselves, Hector was happy with me; happy with a twilight happiness in which to lay his head in my lap was the most he ever asked for. A disembodied love, even though my blood raced at the slightest touch of his lips on my neck; it was an attempt to love differently from the only way my flesh had ever known. There was space for such a love in Hector's infinitely deep eyes, and space in my heart too, among the ruined buildings of Troy on the shores of a Hellespont empty of ships. I knew my new happiness could not last for ever, but for five long years I was able to enjoy the blinding privilege of that golden light.

16

With his fingers interlaced with mine, Hector was walking slowly in the lazy blood-red shadows of evening, during the late summer of our seventh year of war. From beyond the thick garden walls we could hear the resonant voice of Aeneas directing the changing of the guard, but by the lake where the swans were now thinner, one could pretend not to hear. The gloomy call of the war waiting for seven years beyond the wall tolled like a bell to signal each night and start each new day of that still, silent life. When I squeezed his hand harder, Hector looked away.

'I have to talk to you,' he said.

'I know.'

He looked into my eyes. 'Cassandra . . .?'

'No, Callira told me.'

He shook his head. 'That Glaucus should control his tongue.'

'It doesn't matter.'

Without releasing my hand, he sat down on the grass. 'I can't refuse, the Hittites are our last hope. We can't turn down their offer of marriage.'

'I know.'

He looked up at me. I forced a smile. I knew my face showed no emotion.

'So you don't mind?'

'I mind more than I can say. But I know your duty.'

'I shall come to you just the same. I won't leave you or forget you.'

The flame in his eyes was simultaneously passionate and gentle. I touched his cheek and a few loose locks of his long dark hair.

'You would never betray your wife.'

He squeezed my hand and kissed it fiercely. 'Nor can I betray myself. Or you.'

There was nothing more to be said, so I kept silent and pressed my head against his shoulder. 'Shh. Don't think about it, not now. It'll be months before they get here from Hattusa.'

'Not long enough.'

Now even the birds were silent. Only a light wind murmured among the leaves, which would very soon be turning yellow with the slow death that winter brings. The darkening shadows cast by the setting sun swept across the lawn like a sound.

'What does Aeneas say?'

'Listen.'

I opened my ears to the war over the wall and the regular step of the guard. A shouted command, and they broke ranks. Then the voice of Aeneas was interrupted and silenced by an angry wave of sharp pain. My arms tightened round Hector.

Suddenly he was holding me like a vice and pressing me to his chest with the urgency of desperation. Neither of us spoke again before Callira came to my door at sunset to call me, motionless in the twilight with a shawl round her shoulders and her eyes far away, as if she could already hear the slow, relentless approach of the carriage from the shadowy mountains of Anatolia.

The door in the wall opened silently on well-oiled hinges used by seven years of furtive messengers. I watched Hector close the door after himself and it disappeared, hidden among rust-coloured stones and the branches of the wild fig that grew over it. Between us and Mount Ida were only the Scamander river and a secure ford, within range of our own archers. No Greek would ever push so far, and the entire population of Troy could have slipped through this secret door into the shady oblivion of the forest without anyone realizing it. But pride was the ultimate mortar holding the city together, and I let Hector take my hand and guide me towards the dry sandbanks through water that was only now beginning to rise. Soon all the fords would be closed for the winter. The soft whisper of water mingled with the soughing of the trees as we disappeared into their shadow. Finally the sun fell below the horizon, dripping liquid gold on the rocks and firing arrows of light through the branches.

The almost invisible path continued under our feet. Hector never looked back, but my hand was safe in his, and as I walked I could hear the leaves rustling against the hem of my cloak. The green light above us turned the cupola of sky into a roof. Animals were going about their own private concerns in the undergrowth as I followed Hector. Then we came to a clearing and he suddenly stopped. Still holding his hand, I came closer to him and followed his gaze. He was looking at a ruined temple; its roof had fallen in and tentacles of ivy had crept over its decaying walls. Long grass was growing on its crumbling steps and the twisting boughs of a willow were bent over its gutted interior. An abandoned place. I looked questioningly at Hector but he did not react. Then after a long silence he said, 'Do you see the house?'

Four stone walls, and on the threshold the skeleton of a dead tree. 'What is this place?'

'Somewhere I used to come, long ago.' He released my hand and slowly climbed the steps to the ruin, stopping at the entrance with his eyes closed as if trying to recapture an elusive memory. Then suddenly he looked up and walked in. I followed. The interior was in an even worse state; beams from the collapsed roof were lying on the floor as the last feeble rays of twilight fell on a simple altar. There were no paintings or statues.

'Who was worshipped here?'

He said nothing. When I turned, he was sitting on the bottom step of the altar studying his hands as if he had no further use for them.

'Hector, what is this place?'

'I was just a boy. Not yet twenty years old, but past fifteen. Accustomed to the forest and its animals. I used to walk through it every day, often with Aeneas. Sometimes we'd spend many days hunting. We'd catch wild horses on the plain beyond the mountain.' He paused, as if searching for the shadow of what he had once been.

'I would come to this place alone. It belonged to a priestess. A foreigner, I think from Crete. She worshipped Mother Earth in this temple which has forgotten her. She spoke our language with a soft accent. She was so beautiful.' He spoke calmly, quietly. 'I used to come here often to see her, then one day the house was empty. She must have had to go back to her own land, after only a short time here. They would send one priestess at a time as a missionary. I don't know which myth their cult was based on.' Hector closed his eyes again and a profound silence fell; the light was now turning blue. 'She never came back. No one else took her place. The disaster in Crete must have claimed her too.'

He had finished his story. I waited in silence, a pale echo of his words lingering on the clear air. His first, strange, love. When he spoke again, it was in a cracked voice. 'I never thought one day I myself would have to go too.'

He turned to me, his eyes shining with sadness.

'You're not going away.'

'But I shall never be able to walk the streets holding you close. It would not be fair to the woman who will come to know me as her husband, even if I pray every day for the carriages to drive on for ever and never reach our door. We will never again be able to sleep together with your head on my shoulder . . .' He bowed his head, and the force of his surrender filled my eyes with tears. I stroked his hair, searching for a consolation that my broken words did not know how to express. He laid his head in my lap and I listened to our tears, his and mine, as we wept gently together while the sky above us darkened and night extended her cloak.

Then I reached for his hand and made him get up. My tears were on his lips, and without looking at him I climbed the steps to the altar until I was above him.

There was not a breath of wind that night and the sky was dominated by white starlight. The altar stone was cold under me, and against me Hector's skin burning hot.

17

The wedding of a prince is an affair of state. The throne room was crowded with braziers and its windows barred, and a mass of courtiers welcomed the Hittite princesses and their retinue. Hector stood by the throne in full armour, wrapped in the dark shadow of his discontent, resembling with his reddened eyes a sombre god of the underworld. Next to him, Aeneas, seething in his own fury, had clenched his teeth like a dog about to bite; I wondered if that gloomy rage could ever be banished from his invariably miserable face. Beside them sat Priam, indifferent, noticing nothing.

Cassandra was not there. I did not know and never would know if she and Aeneas had talked of what had to be, if they had ever shared anything more than the icy politeness and burning looks that bound them together. But I did know for certain that it was a day when the doors of the temple of Apollo would remain closed.

I looked over the horde of inquisitive heads attempting one last time to display what was left of their ancient prosperity, and sought Hector's eyes. They seemed neutral, his pain hidden under a glaze of absent melancholy. It was as if he was not there at all, and I only wished I could be a goddess to eliminate the crowd and caress that face I knew as well as my own. I longed to rescue him from that moment. He was now no more than I had once been, just a piece of meat, a head of cattle: the finest bull in Troy about to be sacrificed in exchange for the Hittite virgin and her brother's war chariots.

Paris trod on my foot and rudely pushed me out of the way. Squeezed into the beautiful ceremonial armour which was now too tight for him, he wanted to be there grinning in the front row. I drew back, imagining Cassandra agonizing in her dark attic while I, once Paris's fine trophy, was standing near him for the first time in years. All that was left of our love was a resentful indifference. When the herald announced the Hittites, I closed my eyes. Like Hector, I wished I wasn't there.

18

A bloody sheet would prove that the royal couple had done their duty, and soon a swollen belly would indicate that the crumbling throne of Asia Minor could hope for an heir. Hector's bride had red hair and green eyes. She was beautiful but too young, barely adolescent. She fled nervously down the corridors like a doe pursued by hunters; and knowing no Greek, could only talk with her own barbarian slave women once the interpreter had left. No one knew how to pronounce her name; they called her Andromache but she would only respond to that name when Hector used it.

After the first night he sent her to live with his sisters, but kept away from me except after dark, so as not to expose her to ridicule. The Hittite woman was unquestionably isolated at the court of Troy. I only saw her once after the wedding, one evening on my way down from the temple of Apollo when she dropped her veil and stared at me with meaningless defiance and a sort of terrified ferocity. I gradually came to realize that she loved Hector heart and soul with the same sort of unreciprocated adolescent love I had once felt for my ghost. But the strong silent love of my morose prince was the only lasting happiness life had granted me, and I smiled at the thought of that lonely child seeing my beauty as a threat to her. I held my head high like a queen. And when I saw her eyes fill with tears as she understood the pointlessness of her distress, I looked away. I was not coward enough to enjoy being gratuitously cruel.

As for the woman Aeneas married, she was never more than a vague phantom to me. They called her Creusa, meaning 'the golden one', but I don't believe she and I ever exchanged a single look. She fell pregnant on their wedding night, after which Aeneas never touched her again. Paris's twin Polyxena, who shared his particular brand of superficial cynicism, liked to call her 'the walking womb' but Creusa paid the highest possible price for her heavy belly. She died giving birth to a fragile child who only lived a month in the icy winds of the next winter. Its father buried the infant outside the walls, with only Hector present. I never saw Aeneas shed a tear; his scowl never altered.

*

Hector was asleep, his great body abandoned to my arms on his narrow bed. His room was unchanged since the first time I'd seen it. Dark shadows fluctuated and lengthened into bizarre shapes in the low trembling flame of the lamp as the oil burned low before dawn. I watched Hector and listened to my heart beating calmly in time with his. His face was tense even in sleep, and I wished I could have smoothed out the deep furrows carved by worry at the corners of his mouth. His long dark hair mixed with mine, locks of the darkest chestnut with copper-coloured curls on the coarse wool coverlet.

Spring was not far off; its scent was in the air, and the singing of the birds in the garden trees hinted at a thaw. There were fewer fires burning among the Greek ships. Agamemnon must have known about the alliance concluded with the Hittites after eight years of siege, because Greek lookouts now patrolled the coast road and parties of Trojans had run into them in the forests of Ida. But apart from this the plain was still empty, the sea abandoned and Greece far away; and their houses on the shore were beginning to show their age. The Scaean Gates were still sealed shut and looked as if they had never been open.

I counted the length of the siege on Hector's face and wondered how he would look in another twenty years. Cassandra made no more prophecies, just silently watched time slipping through her fingers. If I asked her about the dark future her cries had once foretold she would not answer. Lightly touching Hector's neck I prayed to the indulgent spirit that had put him in my path to grant me what I had so long dreamed of in vain: to have someone to grow old with.

A bird broke into song outside the window and I got up, carefully arranging the sheet over Hector's body. The shutter yielded easily to my fingers, and I stood for a long moment watching the last frost adorn the chilly calm of the garden. Then the ground was ripped from under my feet, and as I fell I heard Hector shout my name.

19

I woke hours later, one of the many casualties in the long hospital behind the temple of Apollo. Cassandra was bending over me with a smile.

'You're not dying, don't worry,' she said, offering me a cup of water.

'We're all going to die, stupid,' I answered back, reaching for the cup with my lips. Cassandra gave a short laugh and helped me to drink.

'What did I tell you? You're doing fine.'

I cautiously moved and felt myself with tentative fingers. My right leg was heavily bruised and a dull throbbing suggested it might be better not to touch the side of my head, but I could see clearly.

'What happened?'

'An earthquake,' Cassandra answered casually, placing the cup on the floor.

I could feel my eyes widening in surprise as I stared at her calm expression. 'And you didn't know about it in advance?'

'Of course I did, but none of you would have believed me. But from now on, I think a few people will start to listen to me.'

She briskly collected the cup and pitcher of water and stood up. She had tied her hair back, and looked tired. When I showed surprise she smiled indulgently. 'I've told you before, Helen, don't ask me questions if you don't want to know the answers.' She moved away down the narrow corridor between the lines of stretchers laid on the ground, a small soft figure passing between the injured, some of whom were bleeding and most immobile.

It took me a moment to find my voice again. 'Cassandra! How are the others?'

'My brother's fine,' she said, scarcely turning. 'And the Hittite has just finished bringing her son into the world.'

Slowly and cautiously, I readjusted my body on the strip of cloth under me on the floor. Cassandra watched till I was settled, then hurried briskly away.

Lying stretched out among the dead and dying, I felt as if a space had opened inside me and swallowed my heart and lungs in one single ferocious mouthful. His son! The son I could never have carried, and the child I had left behind.

It was a very quiet day. Some lives finally ended while others slowly clawed their way back to the light, cautious and fearful of every breath of wind. I listened to the emptiness grow wider and my mind went blank as memories and thoughts left me, and I asked myself whether this was death. But it wasn't death, and for five more days I lay there until Callira, who was completely unhurt, came to find me down what was now a wider corridor and held out her hand. 'Come home now, your ladyship.'

I made no protest. Grasping her long pale freckled hand, I pulled myself to my feet like an empty sack. Helen of Sparta, Helen of Troy. I walked down the corridor, a sad alley that led to the light of day.

There were signs of the earthquake everywhere. The walls of the citadel were intact and the palace had scarcely suffered a scratch, but the houses of the lower city had collapsed as if built from straw. Rubble still carpeted the twisting streets. On the beach a pitiless giant seemed to have knocked over the stone houses the Greeks had built, like a capricious child with the pieces of a game, which were now lying spread over the sand. Something sparked back into life inside me, and from high above the plain I looked for traces of Achilles and Diomedes. Had the earth claimed them? But the beach was too far away for me to see; I shook my head and called myself a fool. Callira took my arm again. 'You need to rest. Maybe later . . .'

'No.' I lifted my head before she could say any more. 'Don't call Hector. He has other things to think about.'

Callira's blue eyes grew sad. 'He came to see you every day, but Cassandra wouldn't let him in.'

'Cassandra was right. No more games, Callira.'

She said nothing more. We walked the rest of the way down in silence.

20

I did not look for Hector, nor did he come to me. I waited in my rooms; waiting because I had been able to read Cassandra's prophecy in her rapid steps. The peace was over, and soon Ares would no longer slumber beneath the sandy plain.

Like a tortoise retiring into her shell, I vanished into my long clothes and solitary garden walks, no longer climbing the slippery cobbles to the temple of Apollo and its polluted peace. Cassandra sent me messages during that long earthquake-ridden summer, but Callira was my only companion, and it was she who told me about Scamandrius, Hector's son. He had fine dark hair; his eyes were as pale as the eyes of mountain Hittites but deep and wise, and his childish expression reflected the uncertain destiny of our times. I shrugged my shoulders and went on weaving, asking myself whether those cubits of cloth could ever be anything more than a huge shroud for all my dreams.

Autumn came, bringing with it the last aftershock. I stood in the courtyard waiting for it to end, warned as always by Cassandra; these were light tremors, as if the earth were stretching herself, to be ready for her long winter sleep. I had long been in the habit of keeping my more valuable possessions in chests padded with wool and now, wrapped in nothing but a shawl, I faced the brusque reawakening of the earth as nothing worse than an irritating habit. Like me, the Trojan court was waiting, but an invisible wall separated us, the Trojans caught asleep with disordered hair and swollen eyes, while the foreign women, Callira and I, stood motionless near the outer wall.

I could see the royal family grouped near the stairs; Polyxena's long hair impeccable even in the light haze, and her tunic arranged in perfect folds as she chattered uninhibitedly with her sisters. Somewhere beyond the screen formed by the daughters of Priam stood Andromache; I could imagine her pale complexion in the dawn; perhaps she was holding little Scamandrius in her arms, unwilling to entrust him to a slave girl. My gaze wandered across the empty pavement between us, and I felt a sense of loss as I watched that great imperfect family with which my own had never assimilated.

I tried and failed to imagine myself in Polyxena's place, with the lovely Leda beside me, perfumed with the essences she sprinkled among her bedclothes; and for a moment I thought I saw Castor and Pollux among the guard drawn up at the gate – with their closed helms and fierce looks those men could have been Spartans, and this city lost in mist could have been Sparta. But earthquakes had never shaken the Peloponnese, and nothing was left now of my family but ashes blown on the winds. Only Hermione still carried in her veins the blood of Leda and Tyndareus, of Castor and Pollux, and I wondered whether she was at least a little like them, carrying stamped on her face that remote parentage, a heredity of centuries written in the features of a child. Child? A girl now, almost a woman. Who knows, perhaps by now with Menelaus absent they had already married her off, but to whom? All the young men of Greece had been passing the best years of their lives before the walls of Troy.

Lost among my family ghosts, I did not notice Hector until I heard the familiar warmth of his voice behind me. 'Helen.'

'Prince.'

I didn't look at him, I didn't want to look at my sad

love, I didn't want to find out if I still had the strength not to come after him. I could see the sky brightening, and the sharp edge of the wall, the promise of dawn climbing up it with a far-off golden sparkle.

'Helen.' That huskiness I knew so well; I could hear he had come closer, head bent and shoulders bowed, his lips near my hair. Desperate for safety and sunlight, none of the others were watching us, and even Callira had moved away in silence.

'Go away.'

'Helen ...' The half-suppressed sob at the end of my name was too much for me; the precarious centre of my world collapsed and I closed my eyes.

My voice was a thread. 'For the sake of Scamandrius,' I murmured, 'please go away.'

His was even thinner thread. 'No.' His authority was like a rock beneath the waves, and I knew he would not move. I didn't turn.

'I've missed you.' I frowned and gripped my own shoulders as if it was all I could do to hold myself together. He didn't touch me, but I could feel his breath on my neck, and it was as if he had got under my skin and touched my heart with a warmth beyond words now we were no longer able to touch physically in public.

'A message has come,' Hector said quietly. 'Signed by Agamemnon. Challenging us to battle.'

'When?'

'The first day of autumn, at daybreak.'

'So at last he's had enough.'

'He's not the only one.'

'What does the king say?'

'He says I can go.'

I nodded, not trusting the voice knotted into a lump in my throat.

'Helen . . .' But he said no more. I felt his warmth vanish and heard his steps move away. Opening my eyes, I saw that the promise of the dawn had matured into a veil of rose and yellow reaching to the horizon. But the soft light on my eyes could not warm me. When I turned, Hector was climbing the stairs to the palace, head bowed. Aeneas was following with his mouth pursed and his hands tense as if already grasping his sword. My prince looked round and found my eyes, so far away across that deserted courtyard. I nodded slowly; an imperceptible gesture, but he caught it and for a moment I could see anticipation of the day that must come carved on his features. His death was a black shadow round the corner of the road, but there was no despair; only the shadow of a smile with a hint of mist about it.

It took six days to get the Trojan army ready. On the morning of the seventh I woke in Hector's bed to find him gone, and sword, shield, helmet and spear vanished from the walls. I stayed in bed; there was a dusty new light on the coverlet. Birds were singing against a sick sound of far-off marching that echoed from the bare walls, hitting me like a hammer between head and heart. I was a ghost in that empty room, its sad light heavy with a long history of desertion. I hugged my shoulders, trying to remember the touch of my prince in the noiseless night, but I could only feel the delicate chill of the still air. Closing the door behind me when I left was like setting the seal on a story already concluded.

21

Some say an army ready for battle is like a serpent, some that it's like a storm at sea, others that it's like a shower of black pearls, but the fact is its members are all men and all poets. I gripped the battlements and looked down, and all I could see was ants. Tired ants in unfamiliar armour, exhausted by unfought war and endless siege. There was no hatred on the faces of the Trojans, and on the faces of the Greeks only a blind desperation. I don't know who gave the command, but suddenly the Trojan cavalry charged, Hector's black steed leading like a fragment of obsidian; then the Greek charioteers hit back at a gallop, deeply scarring the sandy plain. The cracked earth vanished beneath hooves and wheels as the armies collided, becoming indistinguishable in the dust.

*

The battle raged for two days, after which the Trojans stayed outside the city and set up camp halfway across the plain. Hector sent a messenger instructing us to stay where we were but to gather the royal guard at the Scaean Gates, which had stayed open; he also brought encouraging rumours of disagreements among the Greeks.

'One day of war and they're already at loggerheads,' laughed Paris loudly; he had come back with the messenger, recalled to the city by his need for wine and whores.

'We're winning, Father. Easy!'

Priam nodded, scarcely listening. The skin stretched over his bones was now like fragile parchment. The imposing man who had once assessed me like a cut of meat had gone, and even lechery had faded from his eyes.

'You want we bring tents?' murmured Andromache behind me. She still spoke broken Greek with a guttural accent, though in two years her childish face had grown more sophisticated and embittered. She was holding Scamandrius by the hand.

Paris shook his head. 'Hector says no. He's afraid the Greeks may try a sortie if they see civilians emerging from the city. It would help the hostages. Stay here, little sister.'

He smiled with that smile I knew so well, like a shadow

on his plump overindulged face. Andromache looked away disdainfully and withdrew, taking the child with her. Hecuba followed, and as the court dispersed, Paris suggested a quick toast to victory. Searching the far end of the room for Callira, I quickly came out into the corridor. In the shadowy gloom beyond the torchlight someone grabbed my wrist.

I turned. Even in the dark I could see Cassandra's eyes were wide with fear. Her hand on my wrist was like a claw.

'Tomorrow,' she whispered. 'Tomorrow, the disaster. There's no escaping it.' Her voice was tremulous and distant like the sighing of the wind, yet racked by agony.

'Cassandra . . .'

She gripped me harder. 'You . . . tell him.'

Then she turned and vanished into the shadows. Callira, behind me, looked confused, but suddenly the walls closed round me like black snakes, and my throat was locked.

'Can the Fates really move so fast?' I asked in a choked voice, but no answer came. I pulled my shawl more tightly round my shoulders and ran through deserted corridors and across the black well of the courtyard to the gates. Suddenly I was outside. There was no light, just a sharp, jagged sickle of moon hanging in the sky. I didn't see Aeneas until I ran into him.

'Helen, what's the hurry?'

'Cassandra,' I whispered breathlessly. The familiar grief and anger veiled his face, but he controlled himself. 'Is she all right?'

I nodded. 'But she says I must speak to Hector, that tomorrow—'

'I know,' he interrupted almost brutally, and in the dim light I saw his face grow tense. 'Cassandra told me . . . last night.'

He looked at me with a sort of painful defiance, but I said nothing. It wasn't my business and I had no wish to ask. If other farewells had been said in the dark before the battle, that was not for me to know.

'All she can see is this death, and that there's no escaping it,' Aeneas murmured in a rough, bitter voice. 'If she'd only told me—'

'I have to see him,' I interrupted, suffocated by a sense of urgency.

It was as if the moon was hidden by a thick veil, with night oppressing me from all sides. I had to go, if only to say goodbye. Aeneas understood at once. 'Ride with me.'

Without waiting for an answer he went out of the gates, sentries saluting him in hoarse voices. I turned, and with a quick nod to Callira who was on the stairs, hurried to follow. A guard was holding Aeneas's horse by the bridle.

'But why . . .?'

'The Hittites have sent a courier,' said Aeneas, arranging the saddle with a rough gesture. 'They've swum the Scamander to reach the camp as quickly as possible. They're nine days' march away.'

'Nine days . . .'

'We've spent nine years shut up inside the walls,' said Aeneas bitterly. 'And now we can't even afford to wait nine days.'

He grabbed me by the waist and hoisted me into the saddle, then mounted behind me. Troy passed us at a rapid trot; quiet streets with people leaning from their windows to look at the great wound of the Scaean Gates, open again after being closed for nine years.

Aeneas against me was one single compact knot of tension; we did not speak as we passed through the gates and reached the plain with clouds of sand and earth thrown up by the hooves of our racing horse. A huge fire had been lit outside the gates, guarded by twenty men, and beyond a brief space reconquered by shadow I could make out the bivouacs of the camp. For a moment stars appeared above our heads and the two rivers that flanked the plain, before the fires reappeared and blotted out everything beyond their own pale field of light. A reddish glow against the perfect blue of the sky. Aeneas dismounted at the edge of the encampment and helped me down. Before I could get my bearings he was already leading me into the centre of the camp. We passed through the mass of tents, far from the lights of the bivouac, and soon Aeneas was pushing me through the entrance to a tent no different from all the others, no larger or more beautiful.

'What does my father say . . .?' Hector looked up and saw me. First he looked astonished, then angry, and then with a couple of steps he was at my side. I stood still, uncertain of my reception. But in the weak penumbra of the oil lamp he took me in his arms and hugged me, and for a long moment nothing existed but the drumming of his heart against mine and his dusty hair in my eyes. Then we moved apart, but he didn't release me.

He looked exhausted, as if he had lived through a hundred years in a single day. At last this was war; this was what he had wished for and searched for through all the long inglorious years of the siege. His face seemed to have developed another layer of skin. He had a wound on his right shoulder, but beyond that nothing but scratches, even if the shield propped on the ground had been damaged by new dents.

'You didn't say goodbye before you went,' I said, but instead of the bitter reproach I had intended, all I could summon up was the tremor of tears. I suddenly felt ashamed, a fool in a place where I should never have been, as I looked at our huge shadows on the cloth wall, two human beings reduced to mere twisted hunchbacked shadows.

Hector said nothing but hugged me again, and still holding me made me sit down on a mat. A mat, a coverlet and his weapons; Hector's tent was just like his room, and to one who had spent so much of her life chasing purple and gold, that now meant nothing. When he held me in his arms I wanted only to lose myself, to bury myself in him and never leave him, to be inside him like a second heart. I pulled back from him and gazed at him, stroking his face. 'My love.'

The words were so simple, saying them came so naturally, and the quivering flame threw deep shadows in his eyes. He took my hand and kissed it. I studied his bent head and the powerful curve of his neck, passed my fingers through the loose hair tumbling down his back and smiled.

'Tired horse,' I sighed, winding his hair round my fingers and gently clearing it of dust and twigs. He did not object, and with his back to me I said softly, 'Don't go tomorrow.'

He stiffened, but did not speak.

'Don't go,' I repeated. 'Come back into the city. Cassandra has spoken, she says it'll be tomorrow. That from tomorrow there can be no turning back.'

'The time for turning back has gone, Helen,' he said coldly. 'Tomorrow, or the day after . . . I must go forward, until I find the road blocked by my own ashes.'

I dropped the hair I had tidied and let my hands fall on my lap. My useless hands. 'Don't you believe Cassandra?'

He turned. His expression was grim. 'I believe her. But you more than anyone should know me well enough to realize that I can't stop.'

There was nothing more to say. My hands moved over his face, his temples, his hair, and stroked them as if trying to learn them by heart, to be able to remember them for ever in my skin.

'My love,' I repeated, saying farewell not only to him but to all those I had lost and found and consumed, up to this war and this eve of battle, on this silent starry night, at the same time opaque and sharp, out here on this plain.

Hector said no more, but I knew what was in his mind when his lips found mine. It was not a kiss, barely a caress.

He got to his feet, towering over me in the low tent, and held out his hand. I grasped his familiar rough palm and stood up, and he embraced me for the last time as if he still hoped somehow to put off the moment of my leaving, of my being swallowed up again in the darkness beyond the oasis of light that was the tent. We stole one more moment from the Fates, his skin and mine close together for a last fragment of time, then, without looking back, I pushed aside the flap of the tent and felt cold sand invade my sandals and caress my feet.

Aeneas was sitting on the ground outside, and when he saw me he got up and without asking questions showed me the way to his horse. When I looked back, Hector was standing at the entrance to the tent, dark and tall against the black interior surrounding him like a soft halo. I wanted to run and collapse like a falling tower into his arms, to throw myself on the ground and weep and howl and beg him to come home with me to the city walls and their illusory protection, to the monotony of our lost sunsets in the cold of the siege; but I did nothing. My bones full of lead, my heart heavy with iron in my veins, I turned away, tearing my soul up by the roots like a tree. He did not move, himself immobilized by that light and that moment, by that last heavy duty. Aeneas was waiting for me outside the cone of shadow, and his horse was ready. I mounted in silence, and when the horse moved I knew without looking that he had already gone back inside. We're made of stone.

The return journey took a century yet passed in a split second; everything was far away and out of focus, yet at the same time sharp and strangely distinct, as if outlined by an inexperienced painter in black. We passed the fire and entered the Scaean Gates, the familiar uphill streets ran by under the horse's hooves, and it was not until we reached the courtyard that I realized I had never looked towards the fortifications and the Greeks on the other side of them. It was as if they had had no existence, though they too were part of the darkness and the silent black menace of the night. Aeneas took leave of me with a glance and a simple gesture, his horse already handed to a guard. Callira emerged from the shadows of the colonnade, her face full of mute questions. I shook my head to forestall her, and watched Aeneas pass through the gate, absolutely certain of the route he had to take in the bluish light, towards the hillside and up to its white temple, and the restless priestess who prophesied doom but no longer had the strength to lament it. Framed by a pale halo edged with an unwholesome iridescence, the moon was setting.

22

Troy woke at dawn with her gates open and the plain once more under Trojan control. A crowd was manning the bastions, men hanging like bunches of grapes from precarious ladders. Happy faces everywhere, preparing themselves for battle as if for a play they had already seen, its conclusion foregone. Standing aside, I watched the Trojans dismantle their camp, and the Greeks open the double doors of their own wall. Getting ready for battle as for a day at work, their movements marked with the unthinking repetition of a ritual learnt by heart.

Cassandra was at my shoulder. 'Watch my prophecies come true, Greek woman. Victory will be followed by defeat, and every defeat will be a new victory.'

The dust was agitated, down there on the plain, victory and defeat spiralling together in a confused dance.

*

The Trojans broke through the Greek defences. We saw them charge at the double through the wide open gate in the wall; charge, and pass between the houses like the shadow of a storm, dividing and spreading in streams among the stone camp buildings, as far as the beach and the pale foaming edge of the sea. Ants, or better, wolves.

Flowers of fire and leaves of smoke blossomed in the clear morning air as the Greek ships went up in flames, and with them their hopes of getting home. I could not hear Hector's triumphant cry as he watched the ships burn, but a profound and painful suggestion of it reached deep into my vitals. As I clung to the bastions, blood raging furiously in my veins for this victory at the edge of the sea, one day of victory after nine years of war, I could imagine the face of Hector the exterminator before me, ferocious joy twisting the features under his helm, the raw power of his arm scorched with dust and blood and sweat, holding his breath as he raged and fought, Aeneas beside him, leading the Trojans like two demons of the underworld, forgotten figures from beyond the grave at the head of their warriors.

According to Aeneas, it was now that Patroclus came forward, with the Myrmidons of Achilles dropping back as the routed Greeks were forced to face their enemies on two sides; and I can see the Myrmidons in their black armour amid the smoke and dust, struggling against an oppressive cloud of victorious Trojans; and I see Achilles, marked with the same terrifying signs of blood and fear as Hector, death not far behind him. The voice of Aeneas did not tremble when he reported this; and it was later, in the evening, when the Scaean Gates had been closed and the disaster had happened and triumph had been transformed into defeat as Cassandra had so clearly predicted, that Aeneas in the hall in Troy told the story of the cries and blood of battle as the armies fought inch by inch with no longer any definite front line; hand to hand, sword to sword, one single slaughter, a massacre with no room to hurl a javelin and only short daggers able to perform their underhand work. The outcome to be declared only later when it was over, after an exact count among the towering heaps of the dead; it was in this formless chaos that Hector found himself face to face with Patroclus.

I never met Patroclus so I cannot remember him, but I can see him with Hector's eyes as just another soldier; and I can feel the feeble resistance of his flesh to the point of Hector's sword, just one more dead man weighing down a blade already blackened by the blood of others.

I can see him with Hector's eyes, but I weep for him with the voice of Achilles, because I did know Achilles, and knew him as a great and passionate lover; and it is as Achilles that I hear Aeneas, Greek words failing him, describing how Achilles saw his friend and cousin fall; and with Achilles' ears I hear the soft, strangely dull thud as the inert body of Patroclus hit the ground, trapped in bronze armour too big for him, a father's armour too heavy for the immature body of a son going to war. Patroclus left Greece as a child in the retinue of his cousin Achilles, and it will be in the voice of Ulysses, later, that the gentle young face of Patroclus will emerge, a face so different from that of Achilles, his young eyes desperate to see approval on the faces of those round him, heroes already famous, experienced veterans of many wars. Patroclus was very young, and like all young men was excited by war. Convinced that somewhere among the dust, spilt blood and entrails, could be found that scrap of straw, that useless bauble, that object of foolish desire: glory – an empty and sinister word to my ears. It is with Patroclus's eyes that I see Hector, Prince of Troy; and with Patroclus's legs that I run to meet him with my sword drawn.

No, I never knew Patroclus, but I can see him in my imagination and weep for him in my heart, because when he fell he took my own destiny with him, tipping the scales and causing the wrath of Achilles to overwhelm the Trojan army. Poets will tell the tale and no one will believe them, but I listen to Aeneas re-creating the anger of the Myrmidons at the loss of their child companion, so innocent despite his sword and armour in the midst of that siege conducted by men specially born to fight that unique war. A victory turned into defeat; with the sea ever further from Aeneas's eyes as Hector orders the retreat; and the dust settles as the Greeks recover their nerve and launch themselves into the breach with the Myrmidons at their head, pushing the Trojans back beyond the port and across the plain, while the open Scaean Gates welcome fugitives and Paris's bowmen are the first to reach safety. Seen from the walls, the settling dust is like the calming of an angry cloud. The dead are still lying there, too many of them; and the sand lining the long road through the Greek camp has turned to a black pulp, while the ships are consumed by flowers of fire that close their petals in a gentle yawn. It is no surprise that the birds in the forests of Ida are silent, while there among the mass of bodies close to the shore Patroclus lies sleeping for ever, his childish face hidden by the rim of his helm, his arms flung wide. A muse weeping over his body, but the dead have no eyes to see her.

23

It was as if there were no stairs under my feet. I devoured them four at a time in the urgency of my fear, my heart hammering until I could feel the cobbles under my sandals and found myself by the Scaean Gates which had just been closed. The Trojan army was gathered in the square just inside the gates, friends and brothers behind the same mask of dust and sweat, swords lowered and shields hanging loosely from tired arms.

Hector had been the last to come in and was nearest the gates; the great crest of his blood-smeared helm unmistakable. I ran to him, letting nothing physical or mental hold me back, thrusting aside soldiers who stared at me in astonishment, until with the last of my strength I fell into his filthy arms. He said nothing, not even taking off his helm, just held me close with trembling arms. His armour pressed painfully against my skin which was scantily covered by expensive clothes, but I did not complain. When he finally drew back I searched the eyes in the shadow of his helm, but they were empty.

'He was a child,' he murmured, shaking his head. 'The blood of innocents has to be paid for.'

I heard him say that in the shadow of the Scaean Gates. He said it as though it were obvious, a prophecy I had not been aware of when I had seen those gates closed nine years earlier. It was the end, and Hector was already speaking with the muffled conviction of a voice from another world, with no weeping or lamentation. I reached out to grasp his massive wrist, needing to feel its warmth, its assurance of life. But his warmth seemed superficial, under the skin nothing but an empty shell. He held my gaze, but with nothing but acceptance and resignation in his eyes. Cassandra had been right.

'Hector!' It was the unmistakable voice of Andromache. We turned to see her standing a little way from the cobbles, where the crowd was now beginning to disperse. She had raised her veil and was carrying her child in her arms like a shield. There was nothing childish in her face any more. Hector looked at her for a moment, and my fingers gently loosened their hold and released him. He gave me a look of gratitude which I acknowledged with an almost imperceptible nod. A couple of paces and he was with them, taking the tiny proud woman and the child in his arms. The little boy burst into tears at the terrifying sight of the grim man. At that moment there was a strange silence as though a cover had been thrown over everything in the square, and the child's weeping slashed it like a sword. Hector slowly took off his helm and placed it on the ground, and when Scamandrius stopped crying I could see that his eyes were turquoise in colour, and as big as his father's. Hector lifted him up high without speaking, as if offering him to some unknown god, the child watching him in silence. With the square now almost empty of soldiers, Hector finally gave the child back to his mother. His dirty dust-streaked hand lingered a moment on the child's white cheek as he gazed into his son's eyes.

A hereditary link impossible to express in words passed instantaneously between father and son, and I prayed that Scamandrius would develop and flourish, and grow up to fill Hector's armour without ever wearing it, and live a long life in a world without war. But I had no idea which gods his father had consecrated him to, and it was not a subject I could discuss. Then Hector fixed his eyes on Andromache, and, with her eyes strangely unfocused and half-open lips, I thought for a moment she was about to speak, but if there were any words on the tip of her tongue she did not know how to get them out. Finally fear got the better of her proud features and she stayed silent. Hector bent and softly, gently, kissed her on the lips. Then he turned away from her, and it was as if darkness had swallowed up the motionless woman and child, as if they were suddenly hundreds of miles away. Hector had already started saying his farewells, as if preparing to leave this world in calm and silence.

He came to me with his helm under his arm, and took my hand. We walked slowly past Andromache, whose face was once more hidden behind her veil, and walked hand in hand through the streets of Troy until we reached the citadel.

Above us the sun was shining; my white dress was stained with dust and the blood of other people, but I didn't care. I walked with my head held high. Nothing to be ashamed of. Let others gossip and call me Helen the bitch, but on this day of bright sunlight I belonged to Hector. He said nothing, but walked with me through the city streets in silence, passing ruined buildings and flags of mourning faded by the sun. He never once looked back at the woman and child standing at the foot of the road, and I'm certain he never saw them again.

Cassandra threw herself into Hector's arms without speaking. That evening she, Aeneas and Hector came to eat in my room overlooking the garden. Callira served us in silence then disappeared into the shadows on her way to the barracks and her Glaucus, who next day would be facing a new battle and a new war. The lights were low and the night clear, and as we ate Cassandra sometimes looked up and gazed at Hector, only to drop her eyes again a moment later. I can't remember what we said, but we kept our voices quiet, though that of Aeneas was occasionally choked by sudden anger. We finished our meal, Hector eating the most, then walked in the garden under the stars. Hector and Cassandra led the way in silence, side by side. Aeneas grabbed my arm and forced me to stop.

'D'you think it's going to be tomorrow?'

I looked up at the sky; the stars were brighter than I had ever seen them before. When I nodded, Aeneas shook his head violently like a recalcitrant horse. Barely able to keep his voice under control, he exclaimed, 'How can you stand it? How—'

'We can't share our personal destinies with others, Aeneas,' I said, in a voice as grave and dreamy as Cassandra's when she was prophesying. 'I know this sorrow will echo down the centuries.'

He pursed his lips. 'That's not much comfort.'

I shrugged. 'One day, sooner or later, we shall all flee into the shadows and be together. On the far side of death.'

He looked at me. I looked back at him, but his eyes were like stones. 'But you will weep.'

I smiled. 'One cannot be too wise.'

He nodded slowly, and we walked on in silence. A long way ahead of us, the black shadows of Hector and Cassandra were growing steadily longer in the moonlight, as if soon we could all vanish completely.

24

The sky was a handkerchief, a veil, a shield, a helm over our heads. The stars were tears or perhaps traces of distant fires. But I was seeing everything through eyes full of tears unable to fall, as if I was underwater. I held on to Hector's hand like a rock discovered by chance in the storm during a shipwreck; with the world revolving relentlessly as we lay stretched out on the fresh grass of the lawn. Hector neither spoke nor moved, and our locked hands were our only contact, our only anchor in that cold underwater world. The light from the sky was clear and bright but seemed almost sorrowful, and the pungent bite of the air had made me curl up for warmth and protection against his great body, but I did not move under those stars that seemed at the same time both distant and extremely close as their sharp light pierced my clouded eyes.

Aeneas and Cassandra had left us long before – when I had watched Cassandra looking at Hector, I knew she was seeing him for the last time – and after that Hector and I lay on the grass, ruffled children too tired to pull ourselves together and go to bed, two fallen trees.

'Helen.'

I didn't answer or turn my head, but convulsively squeezed his hand.

'Helen.'

The world became even more opaque as the curtain of water swelled under my eyelids.

'Helen.'

I did not sob, but the salt water brimmed over, streaming silently down my face into the dewy grass.

'Helen.'

Finally I turned my head, searching for his eyes. The sky was cloudless. It was the second night of autumn, still and limpid; as if a god had gathered us like water in the hollow of his hand to watch us weep. And tremble. Hector's eyes had never been deeper, never before so far away. And I realized that I would have been happy to stay there, under those stars, until the end of time. Looking at him.

When his hand stroked my cheek, I was lost. The night seemed infinite under the mantle of its dark goddess, and I knew no more; I had even forgotten my own name in the cold air. I don't remember falling asleep, only his body pressed against mine; and when I woke again the light had turned grey and he had already gone.

Hector died on a sunless day. He died alone, because none of those who loved him were there to help him fasten his armour or pass him his shield. No one stood at the gate to watch him set out, no one took him his horse. Perhaps he looked back for the last time at the palace that had been the home of his ancestors, of his family, of his race, his son and me. Perhaps he was thinking about us all when he turned away for the last time, or perhaps he was thinking of nothing, with his mind as empty as the white sky. Empty because everything was ready now, all finished and arranged, now all that remained for him was to take his horse and go one last time down the road.

I know he will have walked with a calm step. I know he will have looked at Troy spread out before him, half-destroyed by the earthquake but still beautiful. His own Troy. *My mother*. That's what Hector called the city. My mother. The stones were her bones. When he reached the Scaean Gates he won't have hesitated. He will have ordered them to be opened. The guards would not have dared disobey him: he was their commander and their prince. He waited in silence with unseeing eyes for the gates to be opened, not looking back or up at the sky, because that was not where his gods lived; they lived in the forest, in water, earth, and stone, and when they spoke it was like the whistling of the wind, they needed no prayers. Hector's gods sang in the Scamander and the Simoeis on either side of the plain, and in the rustle of leaves in the woods of Ida; they sang while the powerful reflection of the sands beyond the gates spread before his eyes, while he slowly lowered the helm to cover his powerful features and serene expression.

The sentries saw him go out alone, his horse moving with a calm, light step as though it already knew where it had to go.

Achilles was ready, still and silent, bronze against the stained bronze of the sand. He was waiting in his chariot for Hector, in full panoply even before the sun rose. Later the guards reported that Hector had stopped twenty paces from his adversary, and that for a moment they had looked at each other, he and Achilles, without speaking because they had no need of words. Rising above the war, they fixed themselves for ever in the memory of humankind. Two champions; the best warrior from each side, and if kings had backed them up, the war could have ended then and there. But loyalty was not something Achilles understood and Hector thought only of redeeming his guilt, his responsibility for shedding the blood of an innocent; and he was right – the life of Patroclus carried a price branded on our skin in letters of fire.

The two men looked at each other, and recognized in each other's eyes the black features of the Fate that had always pursued them. Hector dismounted from his horse and took up his spear. Achilles got down from his chariot and unsheathed his sword. I'm a woman and I've never fought. I don't understand about duels, and would have understood nothing of this one even if I'd been there to see it. But in the eyes of those who told the tale afterwards, there was a kind of sacred dread.

'They were two gods, lady,' the simple soldiers said, shaking their heads.

If they had been gods, in that perfect moment they would have fought for ever. But they were men, one looking for revenge and the other for expiation. Hector fell to the ground. Achilles turned his horses, and left him on the sand of the plain.

25

I remember Hector's body. A single wound, the point of the spear inserted between neck and shoulder where the skin is soft and death quick and painless. I remember I washed him and dressed him, plaiting for the last time his thick locks of dark hair. I remember his amber-coloured skin lightening as the blood drained away, his features becoming fixed in the eternal rigidity of death. His body was so beautiful, even in death. Everything was beautiful about him, my last, lost love. I remember the subdued weeping of Andromache beside me, and the terrible eyes of Cassandra resting for the last time on her favourite brother. I remember all this, but I can't remember myself; the guards say the Greek bitch ran through the streets and out of the still open Scaean

Gates, and threw herself down in the sand of the plain beside Hector as he lay dying.

Instead I have an incurable scar on my heart, the memory of his deep dark eyes still gleaming in that weak light, the touch of his hand that could no longer grasp mine, the taste of blood on his lips when I bent to kiss him for the last time.

I know he looked back at me for a few moments from the threshold of death; he knew I was there but perhaps he thought I was a dream, or maybe death's final messenger. I remember the slow uneven rattle of his last breath like surf on the shores of a distant sea, a grey veil descending over his eyes, and a hand that must have been mine closing them. I know all this, and I remember the sudden deafening silence of the sky curving over the Trojan plain and the black wall of trees that was backdrop to the end of my dreams; I see again the cloud of dust swallowing the chariot of Achilles who never looked back. I know all this, but I can't see myself, because my memory contains nothing of myself but a motionless empty blackness. As if looking on from a great distance I can just see a woman dressed in white kneeling in the dust beside a dead body, her face as distant as the faces of the gods; I see her throw back her head and tense her throat, and hear again her desperate heart-rending scream.

*

Starting at the base, the flames wrapped the pyre in spirals of fire.

Aeneas had come to fetch me, raising me from the sand of the plain and using his cloak to wipe my blood-stained hands, and to spread the news, ask for a truce, and give orders for wood to be collected in the court-yard for the pyre. It was Aeneas who carried the torch, a long arc of red fire in the cold transparent air, to the base of the bed of wood impregnated with oil.

The Trojan court was drawn up in order, motionless. Cassandra stood straight and slender, her hair made fiery by the light from the flames. Andromache, no longer veiled but barely conscious, was as pale as foam. The face of Aeneas was dark with fury under his helm. My veins no longer ran with blood, but liquid steel. The Kindly Ones were screaming inside me with Nemesis on my shoulder, knife ready in her claw-like fingers, as I watched my last love burn.

When I left the city the moon was high, fuller now than two nights before, a sinister convex moon for the night of my revenge. My feet made no noise on the sand, and I was sustained by the conviction of a duty properly performed. The pyre had burnt itself out many hours before, and the ashes and bones had been collected in a golden urn. I went with Aeneas to bury it in the forest, the urn in my hands, my fingers giving a last caress when Aeneas delicately took it from me and settled it in the black earth of his childhood where it was hidden by ivy and leaves, leaving no sign of his grave. Priam, howling mad as he staggered from room to room, had raised no objection, and silver coins had been mixed with Hector's ashes to pay for his passage to the underworld and make sure the ferryman would not leave him behind.

On the way back, my footsteps and those of Aeneas echoed like funeral drums. He went to Cassandra and I to Callira. I sat for long hours on the edge of my bed with my hands in my lap, useless woman's hands that no one had ever taught to kill. White palms and slender fingers; the soft skin of a woman who had never had to work the earth or lift a sword. Hands too weak, perhaps, for a man but strong enough for me. Deaf to Callira calling me I waited for night, then, throwing a cloak round my shoulders, I left the city by the secret door I had used that afternoon with Aeneas. With death walking at my side, I followed the river as far as the plain; whether my death or another's it was not my privilege to know. But on the sandy soil that night my shadow was darker than usual. The moonlight had raised a light mist from the Scamander, like an irregular stain on the water among the reed beds and on the fords, which lay like half-submerged marine monsters near the surface of the water. I approached the Greek defences, ready, if necessary, to swim the river to get past them. With a dagger in my belt and an unfeeling heart, I went forward with death in my wake and my head held high. It was when I heard an irregular spasmodic thrashing of water like an animal in the final spasms of its death agony, that I saw him. The moon was casting a silver light on the back of Achilles.

26

He called me by name: Helen. Then, with water up to his waist, he came closer to the bank and watched me. I wanted to hate him, but could not. I looked at his face, and he was as close to me as he had ever been. 'You haven't changed.'

'Nor you.' But in fact he had changed; he looked crueller, his handsome face more crafty.

'You're alone,' I said.

'With Hector dead, I have no more enemies.'

'Then what are you here for?'

He fixed his eyes on me. 'For what you have brought me.' When I stepped back, he smiled. 'You haven't even tried to hide your dagger.'

I looked down; the slender blade was reflecting the

light from a now cloudless sky. 'Maybe I was expecting you to kill me.'

'Then you're out of luck, Helen. My time for killing is past; all that is left for me is to accept my own death.'

He pulled himself up on the bank with water running off his body, painfully similar to a forgotten ghost of long ago. His beauty hurt me because it reminded me how much I had left behind.

'So it's death you want?'

He inclined his head; his lips still curved in that strange smile. 'You've been listening to too many stories, Helen, all that stuff about the wrath of Achilles burning up Asia Minor. Last night I was so angry I wanted to tear Hector to pieces with my teeth and eat his heart, and pierce his heels so I could pull him through the dust behind my chariot. But this morning when he came from Troy I knew he was just like me, another lonely man crushed beneath the overwhelming weight of a stupid destiny. So I left him to you. I've lost too much, Helen. I thought I could find oblivion in water, but there is too much blood on my hands, it won't wash off.'

'Did you love Patroclus so much?'

'I loved him as a brother and as a friend. As a lover, as a master, and as the son I've never had.'

'But you do have a child, Achilles.' Stupid, obvious, forgotten words. My anger was dispersing to the far corners of my heart, washed away by the waters of the Scamander as I stood before a man who remembered me from other times. Deep in his eyes, I could see myself again. He looked puzzled for a moment; then understood.

'Hermione?'

I nodded.

He shook his head. 'You should have come away with me, Helen of Troy.' No longer of Sparta, no longer of Greece. Of Troy.

'I know. But it's too late now.'

'It's never too late.'

He moved a step nearer, and suddenly I was afraid. I took out the knife and pointed it at him. He did not stop, but came forward until its slender, almost invisible point just touched his skin, but when I tried to step back he smiled and grabbed my wrist.

'You'd not be much good as a soldier, Helen. When your enemy's near you have to stick your knife in, you can't draw back. You came for revenge, remember; have you already forgotten that Hector died this morning?'

Of course I remembered, and I felt I could never stop seeing his lifeless open eyes. But Achilles was before me and my hand was shaking.

'Lighten the earth for me, Helen of Troy, spirit of fire. Make it lighter for me.'

His lips touched mine and he pulled me close with his left arm round my back; his other hand, still gripping my wrist, lifted and twisted, plunging the blade into his naked flesh as if it had been nothing more than sand. I opened my eyes wide, trying to release the knife, but his arm held me tightly, until his strength ran out and he collapsed on the sand at my feet.

He could hardly breathe but was still smiling.

'Why?'

'Because I don't want to feel any more pain.'

'Then you're a coward, Achilles of Phthia.'

He laughed, and grimaced with pain.

'I haven't much time. Tell me you loved me, Helen.'

I stroked his face and a lock of wet, heavy hair. His hands were lying useless by his sides, hands that a few hours earlier had taken Hector's life. But no grief was crying out inside me, and my heart was calm. The Kindly Ones had been placated; I remembered Hector's smile: *It's him or me, Helen my love, him or me, and in any case he'll soon be joining me. In another world we would have been friends.*

'I believe you,' I murmured to the night, and bent over Achilles, my lips touching his. 'I love you,' I whispered, and it was true. With his death I was burying myself: Helen of Sparta, Helen of Troy, Helen the Foreign Bitch; the world was leaving me, as it left Hector the day before he died. Saying farewell. The pain was a dull useless pulse, and in any case only mine.

Achilles smiled. 'With Patroclus, then, there have been two of you. A lot for one man ... perhaps too much. We'll meet again, Helen of Troy.'

'On the far side of the Styx?'

His smile widened. 'There's no Styx or Acheron, don't believe fairy tales, my sweet darling, my strong spirit of fire.'

He gave a start, squeezed my hand hard and shuddered.

I whispered in his ear, 'Hermione has your eyes.'

When I lifted my head, he was dead. But there was still the shadow of a smile on his lips.

I got up. I had neither the strength nor the inclination to pull out the dagger. I was weightless, as if even the inconstant light of the moon could be enough to carry me off. Next morning when I woke, grief would seize me and rip me to pieces like a wild animal. But not now. I looked towards Troy: the city was dark, enclosed in its own mourning, motionless and proud against a sky whitened by the moon. I began to walk, my shadow stretching obliquely behind me. Now I really was alone. When I reached the loop of the river I looked back. There lay Achilles, stretched on the ground, his arms loose, on his lips that secret smile. In the silver light of the moon he looked like a sleeping god.

27

Two days later it started raining. I scarcely felt the first drop on the skin of my right shoulder. When I looked up the sky was a lake of milk crossed by ragged clouds like dirty lambs. Then came the second and third drops and I held out my arms. Then the occasional drops became an incessant hammering and finally a waterfall, making my hair and clothes grow heavy and stick to my body, until it seemed my very skin had been impregnated, and become smoother and harder. The sky turned grey and then black, and it was not until nightfall that Callira managed to get me to come in. I curled up on my bed like a child and waited, my eyes open to the red light from the brazier. Soon the animal beneath my skin would wake.

From a distance we had watched the flames from the

pyre of Achilles, listened to the mourning of the Greeks and been aware of their funeral games. We heard the noisy lamentations of the Myrmidons as they marched naked across the plain in salute to their leader, their heads strewn with dust, beating their spears on their shields and shouting their war cry until they were hoarse.

I watched them and envied them. I had the blood of Achilles on my hands and carried the memory of Hector behind my eyes, but I could not cry out or weep. For hours I gazed at the sky, listening all night to the rain on the roof, as the drops beat down in the same rhythm as my exhausted heart. A soft rhythm, because it had no energy left. Rather, a dull pain was biting my vitals, dull because there had been too much pain, always too much of it, and by now there was nothing left in me for it to seize and devour.

When next morning Callira came to draw back the curtains on a world still grey with rain, I did not move. She spoke but I hardly listened; I could hear the slow cadenced rhythm of her voice but could not distinguish words. It was only when that subdued music stopped that I opened my mouth. My voice was harsh, as though it had not been used for centuries: 'Why have you never gone away?'

'Because you are all I have, Helen.'

*

Then I must have fallen asleep without realizing it, because I was woken by hammering on the door. Callira's voice rose above the insistent drumming. 'She's asleep! Leave her in peace!'

'Out of my way, slave!'

A blow and a cry. I sat up, not a conscious gesture but a reflex, and by the time Paris broke the door open I was already on my feet. The door struck the wall and bounced back. Through the doorway I could see Callira's legs stretched out on the floor. They were moving, but feebly, and ignoring Paris I rushed towards her. But he grabbed me by the shoulders and pushed me back.

'Not so fast.' He smelt of wine.

I faced him, my previous indifference replaced by calm fury. 'Let me past.'

'No. Your whoring days are over.' He spoke firmly despite the drink.

'You don't know what you're talking about.'

'Your lover's been cremated on his pyre. You'll never see him again.'

'Not true. All I need is to die.'

He gave a mirthless laugh. 'Of course. Hector the hero. The fearless general, the just man. No better than me, when it came to it. He too deceived his wife with the first woman who walked past.'

'Don't talk about things you don't know about and will never understand.'

'It's not worth playing games with me, Helen. I know you too well . . .'

I looked at his face; the face of a stranger, with savage hatred carved into the corners of his mouth. A man I had loved and followed. And now that man didn't exist any more.

'You've never known me, Paris. Lust isn't love. I came here for your sake, and when you grew tired of me, I learned how to live on my own. You have no right to reproach me.'

'No right? What right are you talking about, woman?' He angrily grabbed the table by the wall and overturned it. The pitcher of water was smashed to pieces, and bracelets fell into the widening pool of liquid.

I smiled, scornfully. 'Menelaus never rejected me. But to you I was never anything more than a tart.'

'Not true!' He moved the upset table out of his way and advanced on me, glaring. I held my ground and looked back at him.

'I'm not afraid of you,' I said coldly. 'I've seen worse things than drunk cowards.'

A violent slap caught me on the cheek, knocking me against the edge of the bed. I pulled myself out of his reach, laughing. 'What a pity you didn't put all that manly strength into fighting the Greeks, my dear Trojan prince.'

'Shut up. Silence. How dare you mock me!'

He grabbed my wrist and dragged me along the floor.

'Go on, hit me, don't be afraid.' I was light-headed. What did I care? I was beyond fear. 'I'm only a pathetic unarmed woman, go on.'

He hesitated, staring at me.

'What's the matter?' I taunted him, my cheek throbbing. 'Don't you still find me beautiful, Paris? Surely I'm still the stunning luxury slave girl you got bored with after little more than a year? Worth a war, eh, Paris?'

'For you. To think I did all this for you,' he hissed. 'My people have died for you. My country has been ruined for your sake!'

'For me?' I echoed, unable to believe my ears. 'Oh no. All to suit your own whims, Paris. You stupid, vicious, spoilt child.'

'How dare you!' A second blow thudded into my temple, and I would have been knocked flat if he hadn't been holding me up by the arm. Everything became confused and a terrible pain throbbed in the empty spaces of my head. But Paris was not satisfied.

'You made a laughing stock of me. You and the heir to the throne, the favourite son, the matchless brother

. . . But now your lover's dead, so you're quite right, you're nothing but my tart . . .'

He let go of my arm, but before I had time to pull myself together and get up he was on me, forcing me to my knees, my reflexes too slow, my arms too weak to free myself. When I screamed, it was his turn to laugh.

'Yes . . .' he panted, forcing my thighs apart. 'My tart.'

My cries became a single continuous scream and I pummelled his back, but the bestial grunting in my ears went on until the black outline of another man appeared at the edge of my field of vision. The weight of Paris instantly slipped off me and I lay still.

'You animal! You cowardly beast, get to your feet!'

It was the voice of Aeneas. I forced myself to open my eyes and saw his face twisted with rage. Paris seemed to shrink under the furious glare of Aeneas. His lip was already split, and now Aeneas struck him again without meeting any resistance. His eyes blank, huddled on the floor with his undone clothes hanging off him like rags, Paris began to weep.

Disgusted, Aeneas clenched his fists, ready to strike again.

'Please stop, Aeneas. Let him go,' I whispered with what little voice I still had left. I thought he had not heard, but he hesitated and looked at me. 'It's not worth it,' I breathed, feebly trying to readjust my tunic, but

Aeneas was too quick for me. He knelt down and wrapped me in my shawl, which had been lying on a chair.

'I'll take you to Cassandra,' he murmured, lifting me in his arms. As we turned to go he stopped beside the heap on the floor that was Paris. 'Out of here before I get back.'

Over Aeneas's shoulder I could see a lost expression on Paris's face as he raised his head; he was a child again, a little boy sozzled with wine and beaten too hard. But I had no strength left to pity him. I rested my head on Aeneas's shoulder and closed my eyes.

Callira hurried up before we went outside.

'You were right to call me,' Aeneas reassured her. 'She's all right now. Please tidy up. I'm taking her to Princess Cassandra.'

I would have liked to open my eyes to smile at Callira but I hadn't the strength. Her deft hands pulled my shawl over my head, then I was outside in the rain with Aeneas.

'He loved you.' The voice of that brusque and taciturn man was cracked, like a plain parched by a long drought. 'Don't listen to Paris. He loved you. He was my brother, and you will always be my sister.'

Suddenly my tears came, brought on by the rough loyalty of Aeneas. They overflowed and mingled with the rain. Long soft sobs from my throat made my whole body tremble. The past. The past. The past. It would never again be the present, always the past, until I rejoined him beyond time. The past, the past, the past. Hector, Achilles. Between them and me the shadow of death under this gentle rain. Realizing I was weeping Aeneas stopped, got down on the ground in the rain and laid me beside him. With my eyes closed I hugged him, burying my face in the folds of clothing round his neck. He held me close with furious desperation; I could feel his face pressed against me; though unlike mine his body was not trembling, his heart was beating to a sorrowful rhythm. We lay in the rain on the empty road without moving until we had both finished weeping, and only then did he get to his feet again. I looked at him. My brother indeed. My twin in pain. He offered me his hand to help me up, and when I was back on my feet we walked on up the hill side by side, his arm round my waist so I should not fall, my head on his shoulder.

Cassandra was waiting for us at the top of the steps. My brother and my sister. The rain must have washed away the blood. I was not alone in my grief.

28

The rain slowly measured out the time of truce, and my pain vibrated in time with it. I went about wrapped in spirals of pain as if in a warm woollen shawl, and all was silent; heavy veils covered everything, and no one spoke. Our footsteps on the streets made no noise, and Cassandra bent silent over her altars. Aeneas was silent too, his hands swinging gently at his sides, in his eyes a strange calm. Nothing happened beyond the walls while we waited, trapped in a time warp; not even earthquakes came to disturb us. Everything had been said, the champions were dead, and no one else would ever come to save us.

Andromache had not gone back to her native land; she had stayed with us in Troy, a black veil round her head as a formal symbol of mourning. Paris left me alone, dragging himself like an exhausted cat from room to room and hardly speaking. Priam had gone mad. He sat on his rich throne gazing into space, a shell of a man. Rumours reached us from the Greek camp that Ajax, son of Telamon, a cousin of Achilles, had killed himself. I was not surprised. Death was the whispered theme of our gentle rain, though it was in no hurry; it was waiting patiently and silently for us to come one by one. I was unafraid but not anxious to seek death out; one evening it would come to me with a smile, and would lead me with its cold hand to silent lands far beyond the night, where Hector would be waiting on the shores of the ocean. That would be my death, and that was how it would happen, I thought. Our ghosts were walking with us beneath the porticoes and in the rain-drenched court-yards, as we waited with quiet confidence.

But one morning I woke and found myself full of life. A pale sunbeam from beyond the curtain was resting on my face, and no ships were to be seen any more on the sea or the shore. Not even the few that had escaped the fire. All that was left, on the ravaged earth, were the abandoned huts of the Greeks, like empty shells washed ashore by the waves.

29

We emerged into the sun with the stunned caution of hunted animals after the long lethargic sleep of the sodden earth. The Scaean Gates were beginning to dry out in the pale light, and as we looked up at the sickly sun, we felt a sort of disheartened exhaustion. It couldn't last. We crossed the plain, both old and young from the court of Troy, Callira and I the only women. She supported me with her strong pale arms; and I leaned against her familiar body as though no longer capable of walking, as if compelled to go on living in a world no longer my own.

Then I heard a light rustle beside me, and Cassandra slipped her arm through mine. I gave her a distant smile as we walked together as far as the Greek wall, stopping only just out of range of the archers. But there seemed to be no one behind the fortifications and no arrow cleft the air; only the Greek gates themselves barred our path, still damaged from the time Hector had smashed his way through them.

We waited. Finally, Aeneas, shield on arm, grasped his spear and advanced, hurling it over the wall. It whistled through the air, but no cries responded from the other side. All we heard was a soft thud, as though it had landed on nothing but wet earth. Aeneas had lost his indecisiveness somewhere during that long period of exhaustion, and now he signalled to two men to go back into Troy for engineers. The gates were unbarred without anyone raising a finger to defend them. Once flung open like silent mouths, all they revealed was desolation and emptiness. The streets and pathways of the Greek encampment were deserted, not a dog or a tree to be seen. Not so much as a forgotten rag to be found in the huts when the Trojan soldiers scattered and went in to check. The only thing in the largest open space was a black horse made of wood and covered with pitch, with a thick neck and shapeless muzzle, and mounted on wheels. At its feet were offerings for the gods of wind and sea. We looked at it, its eyeless face just a little higher than a man's head, and all we could hear was the swish of the sea beyond the last row of huts. As we looked at the horse we might have been petrified there, turned to stone by the contagious enchantment of our own melancholy, but the world was not yet so sick, proved when a gull skimmed over the buildings, emitting its graceless cry. As if waking with a start, Aeneas went forward to pull his spear out of the ground and walked round the horse, striking its sides and muzzle. It sounded solid, as if there could be no trick hidden in its great round belly. It was obviously just what it looked like, an offering to the god of the sea to ensure the Greeks a safe journey home.

No one said anything; a murmur rose like a sigh in our throats, but we did not dare to speak. Aeneas strode on with knitted brows and disappeared behind the nearest hut; for a moment he seemed to have slipped between the folds of time into some distant other world. Then his cry rose above the silence of the sea. 'You're free to go!' He came running back towards us. 'You're free to go,' he repeated. 'They're not here any more.'

It took a moment for his voice to penetrate, and another before the buzz from us became a shout, with Paris the first to run past the huts to the shore. I squeezed Callira's wrist, and with her still supporting me I too passed beyond the blind walls of the huts, to see the sea open before me as never before in ten years of war.

Aeneas was right, everything had gone. The embankments designed to protect the ships from the tide had been levelled and nothing was left but the dismantled keels of ships too rotten to be repaired. Apart from occasional washed-up scraps of plank and rope, the waves had already drowned the war wrecks in piles of mud, sand and stones. Soon no trace of the departing Greeks would be left. I looked around: one soldier was kneeling on the ground in tears. Others simply raised their arms to the gods.

I can't say what could be seen on Priam's face if not the madness, so similar to my own, in which he lived enclosed; but Paris ran into the sea, laughing like a child in the shallow water, pouring handfuls of it over his head, and a few of the courtiers who were his usual drinking companions followed.

Callira released my arm and I saw her walk slowly over to Glaucus, a figure much like the other men in armour, though to her unique and unmistakable. Surprised to find I could stand unassisted and was alone, I gazed at the sea. Paris caught my eye and laughed. For a moment in the warp of time the days were turned back, and he was once again the happy boy I had loved in Sparta. Splashing triumphantly, he came back to land, grabbed my wrist and pulled me with him into the water. The wind, now smelling only of salt and not of ashes and war, caught my shawl; and mixed with the laughter of Paris I heard another sound, something rusty and unfamiliar to begin with, but when it recovered its characteristic ring and tinkle I recognized it. It was my own laughter: I was me.

Dancing with Paris I lost my sandals in the heavy sand but I didn't care, skipping about in the water in a way that had never been allowed to me even when I was a child. Suddenly the sky above my head had lightened and moved farther away, and there was nothing covering it but a few transparent scraps of cloud. Looking towards the beach I saw Aeneas; he had taken off his helm and put down his spear. Cassandra was leaning on his shoulder and smiling.

30

They didn't even need to lash the horse to a chariot to drag it inside the walls. Using their bare hands they dragged it through the Scaean Gates which would never be closed again. Heralds were sent along the streets to wake the people with trumpets, and the decimated population of Troy gathered by their hillside homes, on their faces the same unbelieving expressions as had been on our faces that day at dawn. When they saw the horse they believed the heralds had spoken true. I had never before heard a shout like the one that now tore through the air; the triumph of a thousand throats. The people were a hundred-headed Hydra with a single voice. The gods had spoken, and Troy was safe. Prince Paris, now heir to the throne, was borne aloft in triumph. The heroes lay forgotten in their graves and a shadow fell across my weak smile. Remember those you have lost, I wanted to shout, remember the price you have paid for this day. But the living care only for the living, and the dead always have the worst of things. I turned my back on the glory that had been Troy and walked away.

I spent that day sitting among dead leaves in the forest. My legs gathered under me, my arms tensed, my fingers gently caressing the earth, the earth that covered Hector, and where Achilles also lay. They were my dead, and they were near me. The wind whispered softly among the trees. Death had drawn back, and my senses had grown sharper. The air was more fragrant than it had been for a long time, and slow calls reached me from the slopes of Ida, the calls of animals moving in the forest, their savage intensity far removed from me, untouched by human pain. If only I too could have vanished in the slow stream of unconscious, merciful nature; but the only consolation she could offer was this new caress of the earth, which I welcomed on my naked arms. It was night, already dark, when the owls began to hoot and the howling of a wolf made me stretch my legs and rise to my knees; smoothing down my skirt I looked round myself, and felt no fear of the empty forest.

The sun had set on the walls of Troy; it had set for the last time, though I did not know it as I walked slowly down the path, and when I turned I saw that a breath of wind had stirred the leaves and smoothed away the last trace of me on the earth.

When I came out of the forest and could see them again, the stars were shining a long way off and the air was cold.

31

Luckily for me I did not go to bed and sleep. Others were rudely awakened with a sword at their throats, and many never woke at all, or closed their eyes, drunk with wine, and collapsed in the streets round the many bonfires; the Greeks took them by surprise and their lives ended there and then without them even being aware of it. They slipped from sleep to death and never knew the difference. But I was sitting in the garden when fire gripped the lower city, and when I saw the smoke I knew it was not just another bonfire. The air was heavy with ash and the smell of burnt flesh, and when I heard the cries it was impossible to have any more illusions.

'Callira!' I called out loudly in a firm voice, my tiredness forgotten.

She answered from inside. 'Someone's knocked over a lamp. Those drunks . . .'

But when she came to the door I could see terror in her face. Never, never all through those years of war and fear, had Callira ever hesitated. I stepped firmly forward and grabbed her wrist. 'Tell me.'

In the gloom of the garden her eyes were enormous lakes of black shadow. I swallowed, speaking before she had a chance to: 'The Greeks.'

She quickly nodded twice. 'They're back . . . they're inside the walls! I was with Glaucus at the barracks, Prince Aeneas came to wake us, I had to run away . . .'

She looked back at the road leading to the barracks yard where the soldiers must now be taking up their arms, and I could imagine Aeneas falling them in at the gates of the citadel in an attempt to hold this last line of defence . . .

'It was Ulysses,' she said calmly, as though this were obvious. 'They must have hidden themselves with their ships behind Cape Tenedos. We were stupid not to check.' We. Were stupid. Ten years of war. And this city lost. Yes, ours. Our own city. Helen of Troy.

'You've got to escape, Callira. You can't stay here with me. Maybe they haven't found the secret gate. Go that way; or rather no, first go to the temple. Cassandra's bound to have known what would happen. She must have organized an escape route for her priestesses.'

There were no more decisions to make, only paths to follow and destinies to accept. The city was lost. Menelaus would kill me with his sword. A merciful death, certainly. That would be the end; all I had to do was wait. Hector had ridden out through the gates, alone, one last time; Achilles had guided the knife in my hand. A glorious death and a loving death. Now it was my turn, and my death would be quick and just. Punishment for my betrayal and flight. Thirteen years of life stolen from Sparta and its eternal boredom. I had had everything, and now there was this fire. I firmly detached Callira's clinging hands. 'If I am still your lady, you must do what I say. Just go.'

She was hesitating, I could see it in her face, but I too had the blood of kings in my veins and the throne had spoken through me. So Callira, slave and friend, my life companion, indeed the companion of all my many lives, let go of my arm, and with a desperation I knew only too well in myself, kissed my hand. 'Please don't die,' she said.

'We all die sooner or later. But you run off now.'

I slipped a bracelet off my wrist and pressed it into her hands. She didn't put it on, but held it as if it were more precious and fragile than it actually was, and went on looking at me with her head turned, as though hoping or fearing that I might say something more. But I had nothing else to say. At last she spun away and started walking quickly, and when she reached the garden gate she angrily threw it open. Then she was out and safe.

I went back in and closed the door carefully, then sat down on the bed. Outside in the garden the night was clear, but smoke from the fires was hiding more and more of the stars. Troy was burning; one huge pyre. But there would be no urns for the ashes of her dead, and no tombs. Just bare stone and collapsed beams. The gods had abandoned us. There were too many cries for one to distinguish them individually. I listened to my heart which was beating calmly, and my whole life was not passing before my eyes as they say happens to those about to die. Only fragments, shadows and the echoes of voices, and when among thousands of others a particular face reappeared, I knew. That I had come to the end of my road. Death was ready for me. He didn't smile, but I could see his face now. My ghost, my first ghost, was back. His shadow was as long and dark now at the end as it had been at the beginning. He sat down beside me on the bed, and waited.

When Menelaus broke down the door, I was ready. My hair was loose. I had unfastened the brooches of my peplos, which now gathered around my hips. Nothing to come between my wretched little husband and his murderous justice. I waited for his sword; I had learnt how soft human skin is against bronze. I may have been smiling, and when he opened the door, followed in by the fury and smoke of the sacked city and framed by the sinister light, he looked like a demon. But the epoch of the gods was over; now all that was left was man and his miserable work. My hands had been folded in my lap, but now I rested them on the bed. No more defences, Menelaus. But I had spent too much time among great men to remember what cowards were like.

Once Menelaus had struck me. Humiliated me. And I, being strong and self-willed, had not known how to forgive. But now that Helen was smiling and welcoming her death and accepting without question his right to inflict it on her, it was now that Menelaus dropped his sword and threw himself on his knees at my feet, pressing his helmeted head against my stomach. I had to bend down to hear what he was murmuring, but all he was doing was asking my pardon.

I should have laughed; once I would have done so. But now that he was old from war and exhaustion I just took off his helm and cradled his filthy, sweaty head on my breast. It's all right, everything's fine. Fine, fine. When Agamemnon broke into the room with Ulysses and Diomedes, he was the one who laughed. A long derisive, contemptuous laugh. I looked up at him. He was no longer young. His hair was grey and his armour could hardly contain his big stomach. No longer the cruel and fearsome king of my youth, no, just an old man now. I did not bow before the sneers of Agamemnon; on the contrary, I held my head high and smiled. His cruel laughter faded, and I knew at that moment that I would never again be ashamed before these men. I gently pushed Menelaus aside.

'Get up.'

He obeyed and I covered myself while the kings looked away. Only Diomedes kept on watching me. Even behind his helm his eyes were familiar, even after the passing of so many, too many years. But that had been at the beginning of the road that had led to this night and this fire, to this scar, to this infinite curse. The Greek race had been cursed, though they did not know it. Perhaps Diomedes had guessed; one who, like Achilles and Hector and me, had walked in the shadow of death.

'Take her out, Diomedes. Take her to the ships. Then my brother will have his wife back at last.'

Diomedes nodded agreement. Agamemnon, Ulysses and Menelaus went out, leaving Diomedes and me alone in the dark shadows. He didn't look at me, but took me by the arm. I did not turn to say goodbye to my life, and took nothing with me. Let the fire have it all. The light footstep I heard was my ghost drawing back. Not tonight, not yet. I followed the warrior in the crested helm out through the door, into the ruins. Out through the fire and massacre, beyond that death, out of Troy. As we went down the palace stairs I reached for his strong hand, and my flesh remembered it, still knew it by heart. We walked, weeping in silence, away from conflagration and war and towards the sea.

32

There have been too many massacres and they have all been the same, born in blood and dead in blood, suffocated. The mixture of human entrails and black mud kneaded into the earth, and the screams of newborn babes hurled from towers will be heard for centuries. Let the bards tell the story if they want to: the massacre of Troy despite its desperate defence by Aeneas, and his final escape. Not me, no, I have seen too many horrors to accept this as well. I saw Aeneas ordering the retreat, he still had a small band of soldiers with him and he did not recognize me or even see me. But with the courage of common sense he turned and fled. I followed him with my eyes, but Diomedes was running and soon smoke separated me from Aeneas. An old instinct woke again in me to break away and escape one more time. But it was too late. I was too old. Running away was no longer an option. It was all right for Aeneas, but my own last breath of freedom had fled with him into the smoke.

Run, Aeneas, run, on your face the dark conscience of all life that takes form and reason; run; you will lose Cassandra on the way, you will lose your only love, and few other fugitives will follow you, but they will be enough. Your destiny is different, Aeneas; its thread does not end here. But the rest of us are tied to this defeat and this distant, indifferent sky.

I reached the sea with Diomedes and we sat down on the shore. He took off his helm; his face was beautiful and fierce, marked by the years, full of an ancient sadness. My sad, sweet Diomedes. In the end I had needed to find him again to realize that the time I first knew him was when I should have rebelled. A soldier and a tart, once we could have made a strong partnership, but now it didn't matter any more. This was the night of the fire, the last night of Troy's existence; no longer my sign or my destiny, no longer my war. I leaned my head on his shoulder, and there was no more to be said. We linked hands as the waves came in and broke at our feet.

The murmur of the sea drowned the roar of the fire, and for a moment we were able to believe in another time and another world. Together we waited for the dawn.

33

It was strangely glorious, that last dawn. It rose triumphantly from the sea, framed in veils of rose-coloured light. Rosy-fingered Aurora in her golden shawl. The last goddess of that day, of that war. Diomedes got to his feet and picked up his helm. I looked at him: he was already a stranger. Our time was past. Without getting up, I looked at the sea. It was shining pale gold in the early light, but it would have made no sense to say there was no one left to see its splendour.

My story ends with a sacking and plundering that did not involve me. I buried Cassandra with my own hands, helped by a loyal soldier. Her eyes were closed and her face serene. Her clothes had not been violated; just a single blow from a sword across her throat. That was the last thing I did. When they asked me to board the ship, I didn't protest. I only looked back once, feeling nothing. Troy was still there, veiled in smoke. Smoking ruins and unburied corpses. One single pyre. The blackened palace was my last memory. Suddenly the sun was touched with black.

The Ithacans found Hecuba wandering howling on the shore. Wrapped in her dark cloak, she looked from a distance like the emaciated shadow of a black bitch.

I never said goodbye to Diomedes. I hadn't the heart. I caught sight of him as I was going towards the ship. He turned to look at me with dull, extinguished eyes, his mouth tightened in a painful grimace. In the sun of the Trojan shore, he was wrapped in a cloak as if he felt cold.

EPILOGUE

The sun has gone down and the Peloponnese is already in shadow. It's late and the last trace of light is retreating across the dark sea. I hear Menelaus calling from the bows: dinner must be ready, unfamiliar food and unfamiliar wine. When the ship drops anchor this evening, the voyage will be over. For the men on board, the war is no more than a distant memory. I close my eyes again; the caress of the setting sun is a poor consolation. I haven't the strength to face another life. My mirror would only reflect an empty shadow. Memories of my dead are crowding round me, crowding silently round me.

I know the step of my ghost. I waited for him in Troy, but now no longer. This is the moment. I can hear him behind me, and I am not afraid. The sailors take no notice of me; they don't see me climbing up to stand on the ship's side. The shrouds are rough to my hands but it will only take a moment, it won't hurt. I open my eyes wide, and my last memory of the sun is this golden light. When I jump, the air beneath me offers no resistance, and the water closes over my head with the cold embrace of a heavy veil. I'm a seagull on the sea, but I shall rise from it again. When I fly away, they will not see me. This death doesn't hurt, doesn't frighten me. I can see his eyes again in the water, which is his colour. I'm smiling with my eyes open; the salt stings, but it's worth it. There he is, before me. My cremated love has come back to fetch me. I'm still a child and I need him.

Now I can close my eyes, it's over now. Above my head, beyond the water, the last light is an arrow of fire.